To Mars
best
Norma.

SLEEPING DOGS

by

Norma E. Rawlings

Castle of Dreams Books

First impression

Published by

Castle of Dreams Books

8 Pease Street
DARLINGTON
DL1 4EU
UK

☎/🖳 01325 381466

e-mail <u>dreamer@dial.pipex.com</u>

This is a work of fiction, any resemblance to persons, living, or dead, is purely co-incidental.

ISBN 1 86185 215 0

For my children: Neil and Andrea

ACKNOWLEDGEMENTS

Jan Draper – For her help and advice

Mr Dirk Fitz-Hugh – a member of the Anglo-German Family History Society, for his help with the Berlin birth certificates.

The German Embassy – London

LIST OF CHARACTERS

AMY KENDAL	a bank clerk
CAROLINE KENDAL	Amy's grandmother
HENRY KENDAL	Amy's father
PENNY KENDAL	Amy's mother
THOMAS KENDAL	Amy's brother
JOANNA KENDAL	Thomas's wife
LORD & LADY WESTLAKE	Joanna's parents
JOEL BRENT	Amy's boyfriend
FREEMAN & MARIA BRENT	Joel's parents
JAMES & SOFIA BRENT	Joel's brother and sister
JAMES & CHARLOTTE BRENT	Joel's uncle and aunt
JAMES & RACHEL BRENT	Joel's cousins
NEIL SMART	Joel's friend
CHARLES BROWN	a friend of Caroline Kendal
HOWARD MARKHAM	The Prime Minister
GEORGE DAKER	The Home Secretary
DAVID CLAYTON	DCS. Scotland Yard
ANDREW SHAW	Head of Special Branch
PETER MALCOLM	His assistant
DET.SGT. ALLEN	Cropwell CID
DET.CON. HAWKER	Cropwell CID
MR HODGEKISS	Caroline Kendal's Solicitor
MOLLY & RICHARD BENNET	Henry Kendal's neighbours
MR MEYER	a German researcher
JACK OLIVER	a plumber
ERIC BATES	a child abuser
GILES HARPER	Thomas Kendal's secretary
HANNAH	Thomas Kendal's cook/housekeeper
ALBERT	Thomas Kendal's butler/chauffeur
EDWARD & POPPY LANDSDOWNE	friends of Thomas Kendal
LADY SARAH ARMSTRONG	friend of Joanna Kendal
NICO TOLLY	a pop singer
BILL THOMAS	doctor to Henry and Thomas Kendal
GAIL & PETER	staff at Martins Bank
'FRANSISKA'	Henry Kendal's unknown sister

6

PROLOGUE
BERLIN 1943

The little girl was frightened, her blue eyes looked round in her chalk white face. She didn't understand the war, but she knew that the terrible noises outside in the Berlin streets were bombs dropping on the houses.

She was terrified of the noises and the flashes of bright lights and the smoke and the dust.

She sat huddled in the corner of the room, her body covered in dust, her blonde curls matted. A trickle of blood ran down one small arm.

She cried for her father who had gone to heaven when she had been a baby. She cried for her mother who had gone away taking her little brother with her. The child, Fransiska, was being cared for by her Aunt Lilli and Uncle Hans. Her aunt had promised her that after the war her mother would come back for her.

She couldn't find her aunt in the darkness, the dreadful darkness that enveloped her world. She kept calling her name, but she didn't come.

Suddenly there was a huge explosion outside. A flash of light lit up the whole room. The child was able to see her aunt. She was lying on the ground a few feet away. Those few feet seemed like a mile as, with a sob, she crawled over the rubble to reach her. The darkness came again, but she managed to find her aunt's body. She did not see the gaping wound on her aunt's head or see the sightless stare of her eyes.

She snuggled her small childish body against the bulk of her aunt, and clung to her. Her tears were makings little rivers down her dirty face, which ran down into her pale, trembling mouth. She lay there with her body in the darkness, as fear shook her tiny frame.

Suddenly it was over, the dreadful bombing was over. She heard voices. Her body was still trembling as people came into the house, which was still half standing. Fransiska was found by the couple who lived next door, who were friends of her aunt Lilli. They picked her up. They hugged her and kissed away her terror, and they all wept with relief.

A few weeks later, they smuggled the little girl out of Germany and took her to America . . .

CHAPTER ONE
SAD NEWS FOR AMY – APRIL 1990

It was a wet April day. The clouds hung low over Cropwell, a small market town on the borders of Leicestershire and Warwickshire. Shoppers hurried along the wet pavements, their umbrellas bobbing up and down in the falling rain.

Inside Martin's Bank, in the High Street, it was warm and peaceful. Amy Kendal was sitting at her till, serving a customer, when she suddenly felt a tap on her shoulder and heard the rich, deep voice of Joel Brent, the assistant manager. She looked round to see him standing behind her, tall and dark, his brown eyes serious.

"Amy," he said quietly, "there's a phone call for you in my office." Amy was startled, as personal calls were not allowed at work except in an emergency.

She got up from her seat, locked her till, and followed Joel to his office. He closed the door behind her as she picked up the receiver from his desk. "Hello," said Amy nervously. There was apprehension in her mother's voice as she answered her daughter.

"Amy, dear, I'm sorry to ring you at work, but your grandmother Kendal has had a heart attack and is in hospital."

Amy was shocked.

"How bad is she, Mum?" she asked quietly

"She is very poorly, Amy," came back the reply. "Can you come to the hospital after work, dear. She is in the City General in Ward A2. Can you meet us there?" The colour drained out of Amy's lovely face, and one hand went up automatically to her hair, so that she could wind strands of it round her fingers, which she always did when she was nervous or upset.

"Of course I can, Mum." Amy's voice was almost a whisper as she said goodbye to her mother. She was badly shaken. Amy had always adored her grandmother, and they had been very close. Tears welled up in her big blue eyes.

Joel met her outside his office. Seeing her white face beneath the halo of fair hair which fell to her shoulders, he asked

9

her, "What's wrong, Amy? You look as white as a sheet." He put his hands on her shoulders and looked into her face. His kindness touched her, and she fought hard to stop her lips trembling and keep more tears at bay.

"Oh, Joel," she cried "it's my gran, she's had a heart attack and is in hospital. She's very poorly" Her voice was full of anguish. "I...I know you may think I am being silly, but I love her so much. I've been close to her all my life." Joel squeezed her shoulders gently, and smiled into her sad face.

"Of course I don't think you are being silly. We all have people who are more special to us than others. Now you get off to the hospital, there is no need to wait until after work." He handed her a large clean white handkerchief – he knew she would need it.

"Thanks, Joel," she replied with a watery smile. Amy went off to clear her till. She checked her cash, locked her till and handed over her money to the Chief Cashier. She then collected her bag, coat and umbrella from the staff cloakroom. With a heavy heart she left the bank.

When she opened the door she found it was still pouring with rain. The weather was as miserable as she felt. She put up her umbrella and ran to her car, which was parked in the staff car park at the rear of the bank. With shaking fingers she unlocked her Mini, climbed in and switched on the engine, then set off for the hospital.

She drove through the quiet streets, her heart pumping with anxiety. The rain spattered against the windscreen and the wipers swished steadily across the glass, their movements matching the beats of her heart. Amy soon arrived at the hospital.

The car park was full as usual. "Oh, no!" murmured Amy. Her neat eyebrows rose in frustration as she drove round and round looking for a space. Eventually she found one at the far end of the car park. She got out of the car, and hastily locked the door. Raising her umbrella against the driving rain, she ran through the car park until she finally reached the main door. She walked breathlessly through the reception area to the lifts, the rain from her umbrella running unnoticed down her legs and over her shoes, ending in a puddle at her feet. As the lift rose her hand went up to her hair, which the damp air was now making curl.

Amy reached ward A2 and searched for her grandmother, Caroline Kendal. She spotted her parents first, and then caught her breath in shock, hardly recognising her grandmother. The old lady was lying ashen faced in the bed with tubes coming out of all parts of her body, some of them attached to a monitor, which was giving out an ominous bleep.....bleep. Her short white hair was limp on the pillow, and her faded blue eyes were closed. Amy's eyes filled up with tears. "Oh, Gran!" she whispered, her voice filled with disbelief and shock. Her father, Henry, stood up and came over to her and put an arm round her shoulders. "We are so sorry, Amy."

"Dad, what happened?" she cried. When he replied his voice was serious.

"Your gran was in the garden when she collapsed. Fortunately Annie, the nosy next-door neighbour was looking out of the window. She had only just come in. She rang for the ambulance." Amy shuddered. Thank goodness her gran had been seen. If she had collapsed in the house, she could have been dead before anyone found her. What on earth was her gran doing in the garden when it was pouring with rain?

It was a silent Kendal family who sat round Caroline's bed, all deep in their own thoughts. Amy's slim figure was shivering in her blue suit and striped blouse, which was the bank's uniform. Her feet were wet in her navy shoes. Her normally pretty face looked drawn and one hand was twining itself round her hair. She looked at her gran and thought about the times they had shared together. When Amy had been small she used to go and stay with Caroline for a whole weekend in her cottage. She would spend hours playing with her and reading her endless stories that Amy loved. As she got older her gran would take her out for picnics and walks in the summer, and the first week in September it was a ritual when they would walk along the fields picking blackberries. They would then go back to the cottage together and her gran would let her help to make pastry, and they would both laugh as Amy used to get into such a mess. When the pies were cooked she always proudly took one home to show her mother.

As those memories flooded her mind Amy's eyes filled up with tears again as she remembered the times they had had together when Amy had grown up, such as going to the theatre and visiting art galleries or going to the pictures. She would always go to her gran with her tales of woe, as her mother, Penny, was always too busy watching East Enders of Coronation Street on the television. The last couple of years her gran had done a lot of decorating in the cottage, and she had let Amy choose everything. Amy realised, with a lump in her throat, that her gran may have known that her end was near, and wanted the cottage to go to Amy, knowing how much she loved it. Her wet eyes wandered over to her father, who looked so sad. His slim body was slightly bent, his arms were crossed and his glasses were dangling from one of his hands.

Henry Kendal was also thinking of Caroline, his dear mother. She had been a good parent, bringing him up alone couldn't have been easy, but she had always had time for him, and being a schoolteacher she had helped him enormously with his education, and had been so proud of him when he went to university. He looked at his mother's frail body, and remembered how proud he had been of her in his youth. Caroline had been a beautiful young woman, quite tall and striking with lovely blue eyes and golden hair that she would wear swept up on top of her head. She was always beautifully groomed, and Henry had to smile when he thought how many of his teenage pals had fancied her. He rubbed a hand over his head to feel his thinning fair hair, and then looked over at his wife, Penny, who was gazing out of the window.

Penny's thoughts were very different from Henry's and Amy's.

She had never cared much for her mother-in-law. She could remember when she and Henry were young, and she had first met his mother. Penny had been very pretty when she was young, with long brown shining hair that had hung down her back like a curtain, and a slim figure, not like now when she had grown plump and her short hair was growing greyer by the day. She and Henry had been so in love. Henry had been so handsome with his thick fair hair that would start to curl when it got damp, just like Amy's. Penny had loved his serious blue eyes that would light up at the sight of her.

It was when Penny had become pregnant that she had first met the wrath of Caroline. She had been furious because they were both still young. Henry had still been at university and it had been during the summer holidays when Penny had become pregnant. They had got married in the autumn and Penny had lived with her parents until Henry had finished at university. When their first child was born Penny had become a devoted mother. She had taken one look at her beautiful golden haired, blue eyed little son, Thomas, and all thoughts of a career flew out of the window. Penny had loved being a mother and was happy to stay at home. When Henry had finished university Caroline had given them the deposit to buy their house on the Cropwell Road, and Henry had got a job at the Cropwell Infants and Junior School. By the time her little Thomas was at school, and they were financially better off, Penny had been ready for another child. She had loved her little Amy, who had been a good, happy child, much quieter than her lively, loving Thomas.

Caroline had spoilt everything when Amy was born. She had adored her little granddaughter, and sometimes Penny felt sure that there were tears in her eyes when she looked at Amy, who had been a pretty child with blonde curls and blue eyes. She had not been so fond of Thomas for some reason. Being a secretive person she had never talked about her past, so it had come as a surprise to Penny, when one day, when Thomas had done something naughty, that Caroline had glared at him venomously and snapped, "You're just like your grandfather!" Penny had wondered if Henry's father had been cruel. He was never mentioned. Penny looked across at Caroline with her sad hazel eyes. Both her children had Caroline's colouring, but at least Amy had Penny's small teeth and nose! Penny sighed, although she didn't really like Caroline, she had at least always been generous with them all at Christmas and birthdays...

A nurse who walked briskly into the ward and spoke to Henry broke Penny's reverie.

"Mr Kendal, why don't you take your family down to the cafeteria for a nice cup of tea. Your mother is stable at the moment, and there is nothing you can do."

"Very well, nurse, we will, but we would like to come back."

"Of course," she replied.

13

Henry, Penny and Amy walked along to the lifts and made their way down to the cafeteria on the ground floor. Henry and Amy found seats in a corner, whilst Penny went off to the counter where she bought them all tea and some buttered scones, as they had missed lunch. She came back to the table where she handed out the scones and poured the tea. They sat quietly round the table drinking their tea, when Amy suddenly frowned. "Dad," she asked, puzzled, looking up at Henry, "what was Gran doing in the garden when it was pouring with rain?" Her father looked at her and frowned.

"Well, she must have been getting some washing in. At least there was a basket of washing lying on the grass." She looked hard at her father.

"Do you think she will die?"

"I don't know, Amy, but she is old and the heart attack was a massive one." His voice was gentle as he spoke.

Do you think we should tell Thomas?" Amy queried.

"There's not much point," her mother snapped, "she's never liked your brother."

"Now, Penny, don't start," pleaded Henry.

"I'm sorry, Henry," Penny retorted, "but you know how it has always upset me that your mother adored Amy, but never liked Thomas."

Amy began to feel uncomfortable, because she knew it was true. How could her mother be so blind when it came to Thomas? He was older than Amy, a tall fair-haired young man. Many people found him handsome and charming. He was very popular, an up-and-coming MP married to a rich and beautiful wife. However, Thomas had an evil side to him. His smile belied his watchful sapphire eyes. Her grandmother had always been able to see through him. Yes, she could see right through him with her sharp blue eyes that missed nothing. Thomas would not shed a tear over his grandmother's death.

With the weakness of a mother's unconditional love, Penny Kendal adored her son. She had always spoiled him, and he had always been able to twist her round his little finger. She was unable to resist his flattery. She loved Amy, but she was more reserved and serious. "She's left everything to you in her will, you know," Penny said to Amy sharply."

"Mum, this isn't the time to talk about things like that," replied Amy in a shocked whisper.

"I know, dear, but it is a fact. She discussed the matter with your father and me some time ago. Of course, we don't mind. We are quite comfortable, and Thomas is wealthy now, in his own right, but she could have acknowledged him with a small bequest."

Amy was stunned. She had not known this, but she was deeply touched. Her grandmother was not a rich woman, but Amy had always loved her cottage in Bishops Fell, and was pleased that one day it would be hers.

This conversation was irritating Henry. As he stood up his words were sharp. "Come along, we had better get back to the ward."

In the silence and heaviness of Ward A2 they sat quietly beside the bed of the old lady, Caroline Kendal, a beloved old lady. Beloved, at least, by son and granddaughter.

CHAPTER TWO

10, DOWNING STREET – APRIL 1990

The April weather was as bad in London as it was in the provinces. Howard Markham, the Prime Minister, was standing in his office looking out of his window. He was frowning as he watched the rivers of rain chasing each other down the glass.

Howard Markham was a handsome man. He was tall and slim and very smart. His dark hair was smooth with a winged touch of silver at the temples, his nose was long and straight and his mouth was firm, breaking into the most attractive smile which had won him many votes. Howard Markham was very proud of his collection of silk ties. He would always touch his tie when he was worried or nervous. At this moment he was wearing a grey and silver mixed pattern which looked smart with his snow white shirt and charcoal grey suit.

He was waiting, with trepidation, for the arrival of George Daker, the Home Secretary, and three police officers from Scotland Yard. Detective Chief Superintendent David Clayton, Head of C.I.D. Andrew Shaw, Head of Special Branch and his assistant Peter Malcolm. The Prime Minister was concerned at George Daker's sudden request for the interview. Howard Markham knew all the men well, and knew there must be something seriously wrong, for all four of them to want to see him together.

A few minutes later the Prime Minister's secretary showed in the four men. He took their wet raincoats, which they had all been wearing over their suits, then quietly left the office, shutting the door softly behind him. The Home Secretary walked up to the Prime Minister and shook his hand. "Good afternoon, Prime Minister. Thank you for seeing us at such short notice."

George Daker was a confident, intelligent man, tall and thin, with small grey eyes. His dark hair brushed back revealing a noticeable widow's peak. His eyes were sharp, his face lined.

"Good afternoon, George," replied the Prime Minister. He looked at the other men and nodded a greeting as they approached him. They were all very different. David Clayton was the tallest, standing at 6' 3". He was straight backed – a striking figure, with dark hair and eyes and a hooked nose. Andrew Shaw was slightly shorter, a dour Scot. He was a solid, heavy made man with red hair cut in a crew cut, and green eyes. His nose was big and his lips were full covering slightly crooked teeth. Both men were ex-army. Peter Malcolm was different altogether. He was a university man, who had originally trained to be a barrister. He was short and dapper with brown crinkly hair and a brown moustache. His eyes were grey and intelligent. Peter Malcolm was a very clever man, with a mind as sharp as a razor. His interview techniques were so good, he could tie people up in knots. His mild manner and polite charm were deceiving.

"Gentlemen, please do sit down." The Prime Minister waved an arm in the direction of the seats that had been placed on the other side of his desk ready for this meeting. "Well, George, what is all this about?" The Prime Minister began stroking his silk tie, as his apprehension grew.

George Daker looked across at David Clayton. "David, perhaps you would be good enough to explain to the Prime Minister the reason why you came to see me yesterday, and our concerns."

"Of course, Sir," replied David Clayton, who was now sitting with a brief-case on his lap, which he tapped nervously with his fingers. He looked across at the Prime Minister, his eyebrows raised, a note of nervousness in his voice. "You're not going to like this, Prime Minister."

"Go on," replied Howard Markham, "let's hear it."

David Clayton took a deep breath, and began taking some papers out of his briefcase. He put on his large rimless glasses, looked up, and started to speak.

"As you are aware, Prime Minister, it is the intention to provide a National Criminal Intelligence Service, N.C.I.S. which is hoped will be fully operational in the near future."

The Prime Minister nodded. "Go on."

David Clayton continued. "We have begun to recruit personnel for N.C.I.S. and have started feeding the system with details of a variety of crimes and apparent accidental deaths. Following a review of child abusers we have been able to identify a number of cases where child abusers have met with accidental deaths, most of them shortly after their release from prison. We think they were murdered." His eyes narrowed as he watched the Prime Minister, gauging his reaction.

"Good God!" exclaimed Howard Markham. "You can't be serious!" He looked at the stern faces of the men opposite, and stroked his tie. "Perhaps you would be good enough to explain."

"Well, Sir, the first incident seems to be about two years ago, when a little girl was raped and strangled. A local man, Eric Bates, was arrested and taken to court, but during his trial he was released on a technicality. Two weeks later his body was found floating in the Thames. As the man was often seen drunk, it was assumed he had fallen in. A short time later a convicted child abuser was released from prison on the Isle of Wight, his body was found some time later. He had apparently fallen or jumped off Beachy Head. Since then there have been an alarming number of similar incidents."

"Have you no clues at all?" demanded the Prime Minister.

"None, Sir," replied David Clayton," and there seems to be no other connection between them whatsoever."

"Are you trying to tell me that we have a one-man execution squad taking the law into his own hands?" asked the Prime Minister, horrified.

"Not exactly, Sir, it gets worse," replied David Clayton, nodding to Andrew Shaw to take over.

"We are finding members of minority groups dying, in what appears to be accidents. There have been post-offices, chemists and other shops owned by Asians which have burnt down. Other targets are bars and clubs for 'gays', and places for the homeless and down-and-outs, and drug rehabilitation centres."

"My God, this is dreadful!" exclaimed Howard Markham. "Have these proved cases of arson?"

"No, Sir, that's just the problem, they all appear to be genuine accidents, such as faulty wiring, drug addicts who get so high on drugs that they don't know what they are doing, and then there are tramps lighting fires to keep warm. In every case there has been a feasible reason for every incident. Therefore no pattern has emerged until now." Andrew Shaw's red hair was bristling, "Sir, we believe that there must be a group of people

19

who are ridding the country of minority groups. They are being very clever and selective."

By now the Prime Minister was deeply shocked. "Do you have any leads at all?" he asked.

"Not yet, Sir," said David Clayton, "I have some computer print-outs here for you, which you may like to look at. As you will see there is no obvious connection between any of the incidents that we can put out finger on."

Markham took the printouts from Clayton. He was beginning to feel extremely nervous, and picking up his glasses, began tapping them on the desk. "Do you think this has anything to do with the race riots that have started recently?" he asked.

Clayton turned to look at Malcolm, who spoke next. "We think it's possible, Sir. We have been receiving more and more complaints from white people who say that they are being discriminated against in favour of black people. Someone is stirring up the population. We believe their intention is to cause discontent; the result is that fights are breaking out everywhere. We think that someone somewhere is deliberately causing trouble for some purpose of their own."

"This is outrageous," stormed the Prime Minister. "It must be stopped!" He got up and started pacing the floor, rubbing the back of his neck to ease the tension that was building up inside him. He was truly worried by now. This could be a disaster whilst his party was in power. He wanted the best for his country, not to see his countrymen fighting each other. He frowned at the Home Secretary.

"The press haven't got hold of this yet, have they, George?"

"No, Sir, but it won't be long before some smart journalist starts putting two and two together."

I want you to keep this under wraps for as long as possible," stated Howard Markham through narrowed lips. "What action are you taking?"

Clayton looked uncomfortable, as he spoke again. "We are going to start checking back on the families and friends of the victims to see if we can find a connection. It won't be easy, Sir, as most people will not remember where they were at the times in question, and those that can remember may not be able to help."

Clayton cleared his throat, and looked up at the Prime Minister, who was still standing. "Sir, there is more to come."

"What!" snapped the Prime Minister.

David Clayton continued, his hands gripping his briefcase, which was still lying on his lap. "Sir, you will already have heard about the disaster at the new home for disabled children in Westminster?"

The Prime Minster nodded, "I have," he replied.

"Well, Sir, it appears that the home had a faulty heating system, and those children were all gassed."

Howard Markham turned pale. He looked across at David Clayton. "What are you trying to tell me, David?"

"Sir, replied David Clayton, raising his hands," we think we have another Hitler on our hands . . .

CHAPTER THREE

THE DEATH OF CAROLINE KENDALL – APRIL 1990

Caroline Kendal died the following day, having never regained consciousness. Amy was heartbroken and spent the day crying in her bedroom. Her father, Henry, was also very upset. His mother was the only family he had ever known, as his father had been killed in the war before he was born.

Never having had any brothers or sisters, uncles or aunts, cousins or grandparents like his friends, he had had a rather lonely childhood, and now his mother was gone.

Henry was a teacher at the local junior school. It was the beginning of the Easter holidays, and it proved an awful week for him. With a distraught daughter to deal with, a wife who wasn't too sympathetic, and a son who wasn't interested, but pretended he was – he felt pressurised. He had to register his mother's death, which was made more difficult as he had not got her birth certificate, and even after searching her cottage, he still couldn't find it. He couldn't order a copy of it, as he was not sure where she was born, and he was not even sure of the year of her birth either. Then there was the funeral to arrange, and a notice to be put in the local newspaper, and food and drink to be arranged at the Kings Head Pub in Bishops Fell. Friends and family would expect somewhere to meet after the funeral and talk about the old lady.

Caroline had been a teacher in the little village school opposite her cottage, and had been liked and respected by everyone. They would no doubt all attend her funeral.

Penny did, at least, go to the florist and order a wreath from the family. Henry then contacted Mr Hodgekiss, his mother's solicitor. That fulfilled the promise he had made to her months before she died.

The funeral took place the following Friday. The church was small, cold, dark and very old, and heaters had been placed at intervals to keep the congregation warm. It was a bitterly cold, wet Easter, and people sat huddled in coats and scarves, and sat

23

quietly whilst the organ played. The Kendals sat on the front row, their eyes glued to the oak coffin, which was topped with wreaths and sprays of spring flowers.

Amy hardly heard the beautiful service or the hymns or the magnificent address given by Thomas, who was a celebrity in the village. She sat thinking of all the lovely days she had spent with her grandmother and how close they had been. When the service was over she clung to her father. She was a forlorn figure as they followed the coffin to the graveyard at the back of the church where Caroline was to be buried.

As the coffin was lowered into the ground, there was a feeling of great sadness. Henry swallowed the lump in his throat, and even Penny felt sorry and guilty for not caring more.

Thomas stood tall and handsome, his blue eyes troubled. He could never understand why his grandmother had not cared for him, and always felt uneasy when he caught her looking at him with that strange expression, as if he reminded her of someone or something she did not like. He had often been hurt by her attitude.

Amy cried bitterly. The person she had loved most in the whole world was gone, gone so suddenly that Amy had not even had a chance to speak to her, or help look after her. She had just been snatched away from her by fate, and now she was gone forever.

Penny was standing by Thomas and his wife, as Amy was hanging on to her father. Penny was so proud to be standing by her famous son. Thomas looked handsome and elegant in his black suit and tie, his fair hair neatly brushed, his eyes serious, his thin lips set in a firm line. He looked away from Amy, his pretence of grief made him feel uncomfortable when he saw her obvious distress.

His wife, Joanna, stood beside him. She was tall and slim with blue eyes and long golden hair which was blowing softly down her back and round her beautiful face. Her face and figure were perfect, setting off her black designer coat and tall black leather boots. Thomas had met Joanna whilst he was working in London. She came from a wealthy family in the Lake District, the only daughter of Lord and Lady Westlake, whose family had occupied their ancestral mansion for generations. She was everything that Thomas had ever wanted, and he adored her. She also represented the life style he craved, and with her connections had been a great help to him in his career.

Joanna had not the slightest interest in the Kendal family, and couldn't wait to get back to London. She thought that Henry was totally lacking in ambition, teaching in the local infant's school and then moving to the local juniors when he should have been aiming at being a headmaster somewhere else. A job he was quite capable of doing. As for Penny, how stupid and silly she was working in a department store. She also despised Amy's lack of ambition, working in a bank behind a till and not being interested in promotion. Joanna felt herself so superior to everyone she met.

After the funeral, the family and friends went off to the Kings Head. A watery sun was trying to peep through the grey clouds, as they made their way through the village. Everyone was glad to be inside the pub, where it was warm and cosy. The Kings Head was a beautiful old pub with a massive fireplace. A real fire roared out a glowing warmth. The ceilings were low and criss-crossed with heavy oak beams. The windows were small and mullioned, and shining vases of brass and copper, filled with dried flowers, stood on the window ledges. The walls were covered in framed prints of horses and huntsmen.

People started eating and drinking. Feeling the warmth of the fire they all cheered up and started chatting. Thomas came over to Amy and spoke to her. "I'm sorry you are so upset, Amy, I know you loved the old girl. She's left you everything in her will, I understand."

"Yes," Amy replied quietly. "I'm sorry, Thomas, I didn't know until this week. Is there anything from the cottage you would like?"

"No thanks, I don't want anything from the cottage. I don't suppose Gran had much to leave anyway." Amy glared at him.

"No, I don't suppose she had," she muttered under hear breath.

Amy felt such a wreck. Sleep had been a stranger to her most of the week. Her eyes were red and tired from crying, and her face looked pale and drawn. Her usually soft fair hair was lying lank on her shoulders, when normally it would be falling in shining layers. Seeing Joanna with her glorious hair and expensive clothes made Amy feel worse. She would be glad when Thomas and Joanna had gone back to London.

People lingered in the pub, chatting and drinking and making merry. Amy's thoughts were in turmoil. How could people be so happy when her grandmother had just been buried? It was awful – awful! She sat on a chair beside the huge fireplace gazing into the flames, watching them dancing over the coals. Sipping a glass of brandy, she tried to warm her inside and chase away the knot of pain and anguish.

Eventually people started drifting home. Thomas and Joanna came and said goodbye to her before leaving for London, and others gradually left.

The Kendals were the last to leave in a taxi. When they got home Amy went straight to bed. She lay there listening to the wind howling outside and the rain hammering on the window.

With the low moaning of the elements in her ears, Amy slept for the first time that week.

CHAPTER FOUR
A SURPRISE FOR AMY – APRIL-MAY 1990

After the funeral the Kendal family made an attempt to get back to normal. Henry and Penny were worried about Amy. She had taken the death of her grandmother very hard. As it was Saturday Penny decided to take Amy into town. After breakfast they drove into Cropwell. The day was sunny but cold. Spring was in the air, daffodils danced in the breeze and the lambs gambolled in the fields. What a contrast to the sadness in Amy's heart.

After parking the car Penny took Amy to the best hairdressing salon in town to get her hair trimmed and styled. It was then time for coffee and a wander round the shops. Amy bought herself some new clothes to cheer herself up, and then they had lunch in their favourite pub, the Cropwell Arms, chicken rolls, and a glass of wine.

They spent the afternoon shopping and drove home tired and a little happier.

In the evening Henry and Penny took Amy to the cinema to see the latest film, hoping it would take Amy's mind off her grandmother. Afterwards they took her for a Chinese meal where they enjoyed prawn curry, sweet and sour chicken and beef in a black bean sauce, washed down with a light white wine.

On Sunday they all took advantage of a lie-in and had a late breakfast. Later they had a drive out through the beautiful, sunny countryside, stopping for lunch at one of lovely old pubs in the picturesque village of Waltham-on-the-Wolds.

The weekend was soon over and on Monday morning they were all back at work. Henry off to school, Penny off to the department store and Amy to the bank.

When Amy walked in through the staff door Joel greeted her. He smiled at her warmly.

"Hello, Amy, it's good to see you. Nice to have you back."

"Thanks," she smiled. "It was so good of you to give me the whole week off. I was fit for nothing!"

"That's OK," he replied gently.

Joel was pleased to see Amy. He had always liked her. She was so sweet and gentle and pretty and well mannered, so unlike many of the girls who were rather brash and conceited. He had been troubled to see Amy unhappy, and was more than happy to see her back at work.

The staff all made her feel welcome when she got in.

"Hi, Amy, it's good to see you," exclaimed her friend, Gail, giving Amy a hug.

"Thanks, it's good to see you too," she replied with a smile. Even the Chief Cashier had been kind to her.

"Hello, Amy, it's nice to have you back, dear," she had said as she handed Amy her 'float'.

"Amy suddenly felt much happier. She was to be on the tills until lunchtime, and then it was her turn to be on the enquiry desk. The day flew by, as she was kept busy with customers who were always full of questions.

When Amy got home she found a letter waiting for her from the solicitor. He wanted her to see him as his office on the following Friday at 4 p.m. She was to take the letter with her. She knew she would inherit her gran's cottage and her parents had not been surprised when Amy said she would go and live there.

The rest of the week seemed to crawl by, and eventually Friday arrived. Mr Hodgekiss's office was not far from the bank, so Amy walked there from work. She arrived in good time with a mixture of excitement and nervousness bouncing in her stomach, which turned over as she walked through the door. Anticipation was building up in her chest as she was asked to wait.

She found a seat in the small waiting room, and sat, twiddling her hair with nervous fingers, as she watched people wander past the window and noisy traffic trundling along the street. Long rays of sunlight stretched across the room catching dust motes in the air.

Suddenly the receptionist spoke to her, a tall lady wearing large glasses. "Mr Hodgekiss will see you now, Miss Kendal, please follow me."

Amy replied. "Thank you." and followed the very smart lady up a set of winding stairs to his office.

When Amy walked in, Mr Hodgekiss, a tall bespectacled man of middle age, moved across the room and shook her hand. "Good afternoon, Amy," he said smiling. "Do sit down, my dear. You have brought my letter?" She handed it to him.

"Now then," said Mr Hodgekiss, "I suppose you know that your grandmother has left everything to you?"

"Oh, yes," she replied sadly, "my parents told me."

"I have known your grandmother for many years, Amy, and I know she was very fond of you. She was also concerned about your future and you may find her will a bit odd."

Amy looked puzzled, she hadn't expected anything like this. Mr Hodgekiss continued.

"She has left you her cottage and all the contents, and all her money. Her money is tied up in different accounts, so it will be a while before I can settle all her estate, but I do have a cheque here for you to be going on with."

Mr Hodgekiss hesitated, took off his glasses and polished them with a clean handkerchief, then continued.

"Amy, before I give you this cheque, I need to ask you to sign a proviso. It is what your grandmother wanted." Amy looked puzzled.

"What does it say?" she asked frowning.

"Well," he replied slowly, "First of all you must agree to be discreet with the money she has left you. I think she was a little worried that it may spoil your life if it was common knowledge." He hesitated, then said, "The second thing is that you must never, on any account, give any of the money to your brother, Thomas."

Amy sat amazed, she could not believe what she had just heard. "But, why?" she heard herself ask.

"Well, your grandmother, for some reason, did not approve of your brother, and she also felt that he had sufficient money of his own, and did not need any more."

Amy was dumfounded. She had never heard anything like this in her life. In a daze she agreed to sign the document placed before her, and she was handed a cheque, which she also had to sign for. She looked down at the cheque and her eyes widened in amazement – it was for £200,000. She looked up at Mr Hodgekiss.

"Where did my grandmother get all this?" she asked bewildered.

"It is not for me to say, Amy. Let us just say that she made some good investments. There will be further cheques to come, and I will contact you when they are ready."

Amy thanked Mr Hodgekiss. Her mind was in a whirl as she left his office and made her way outside. She walked slowly back to her car, which was parked behind the bank, in a daze. She fumbled in her bag for her car keys, and let herself in. She sat in her seat and closed her eyes. She just could not believe what had happened. Where on earth had her grandmother got all that money? The cheque that was in her bag was just the beginning - how much more was there to come? What on earth was she going to say to her parents? What would they say when they knew she was to have so much money, and they were given nothing? This was awful! If she didn't tell them she would feel guilty. How could she possibly live with her parents and keep such a secret? She would feel so guilty living a lie.

She sat for a long time not knowing what to do. Her slim fingers twisted themselves round strands of her hair. Suddenly she remembered the proviso. She had promised to be discreet with the money. The last thing she must do was to tell anyone. She decided that the best thing to do would be to move in to her grandmother's cottage the next day. Her father had a spare set of keys for the cottage, so she could move in. It would be much easier to cope with this problem if she was on her own.

Her decision made, Amy was ready. With shaking fingers she flicked the key in the ignition, started her car and drove home.

CHAPTER FIVE
MYSTERY – MAY 1990

The next day Amy moved into her new home, Jade Cottage. She had woken that morning with mixed feelings. She had lived in this house ever since she was born. The Kendal's house was a large semi-detached on the main Cropwell Road on the outskirts of the town. Over the years it had been improved with smart double-glazed Georgian windows, a porch at the front and a beautiful conservatory built at the back, which looked out over a large garden of lawns, flowers and trees.

Amy could remember when she was a little girl playing in the garden with her doll's pram and her first little bike, and how she used to wait for her big brother to home from school and play with her. At the bottom of the garden was her father's vegetable plot, and on 5th November he would light them a bonfire there and set off fireworks. Her mother would make hot-dogs and toffee apples, and they would eat them round the bonfire. In the summer Amy would play in her paddling pool, and when her father watered the garden on late summer evenings she would scream with delight as he chased her and soaked her with cold water.

Amy smiled to herself. She had been a happy child, here, and now she was leaving to start life on her own. She looked round her bedroom. It was a mess! She had started packing the night before. She and Penny had gone to the local shop and got some empty cardboard boxes which were now full of Amy's books, tapes, pictures, and all her 'bits and pieces'. Suitcases were full of her clothes and shoes.

She got up and drew the curtains, and looked out of the window. The sun was shining at last, after a whole week of rain. She slipped on her dressing gown and went down to the kitchen, where Henry was sitting at the table reading his morning paper, the Times, and Penny was cooking bacon and eggs. They always had a cooked breakfast at weekends. They enjoyed a family breakfast together, then Amy went up to the bathroom to get showered and dressed, whilst Henry began taking her cases and boxes downstairs.

When she was dressed Amy packed up her toiletries and then helped her father pack the rest of her 'gear' into his car and her own. When everything was packed Amy and her parents set off for Bishops Fell, which was only 10 minutes drive away.

It was a beautiful morning, and as they approached Bishops Fell they could see the village bathed in sunshine. The church spire rose majestically above the trees and windows sparkled in the old stone cottages. The horse riders were out trotting along the grass verges and sheep and lambs were bleating in the fields.

The Kings Head was not yet open, but as they passed they could see that the delivery lorry had arrived and barrels of beer were being rolled down in to the cellar with loud clunks. The landlord was standing in the doorway and waved to them as they passed.

They drove up to the cottage and pulled up by the only door, which was at the side of the building. They emptied the contents from Amy's car, and whilst Henry was unloading his car, Amy and Penny drove off to the nearest supermarket to get food, cleaning materials and black bags.

By the time they got back all Amy's possessions were stacked in the kitchen.

"Would you like us to stay and help you clean up, Amy?" asked Penny.

"No, thanks, Mum, I'll be fine. I've got the whole weekend to settle in."

Henry and Penny kissed their daughter goodbye and left her alone.

As they drove away Henry could see that Penny was looking rather sad.

You'll miss her, won't you?" he asked quietly.

"Yes, I will," replied Penny sadly. Henry smiled.

"Well, now Amy has moved out and we are on our own, we'll have more freedom. How about going to Australia and visiting your sister?" Penny gasped.

"Oh, Henry, that would be wonderful, I'd love to go!"

"I thought we could go during the school holidays, the last two weeks in July and the whole of August." said Henry.

"Oh, yes, that would be perfect, and at that time of the year it won't be too hot." replied Penny happily.

"Right," agreed Henry. "Let's go to the travel agents now."

Penny was so excited she chattered non-stop all the way into the town centre.

Meanwhile Amy was making a start in her new home. She gave a sigh of relief at being on her own, it gave her time to think. The cottage was stuffy, so she opened all the windows to let in the sweet fresh air. Her first job would be to clear her gran's bedroom, so that she could sleep in there that night.

She made a start on clearing out her gran's wardrobes. She would give her clothes to charity. Amy had a little weep as she took her gran's clothes out of the wardrobes and put them into black bags. She got a cardboard box in which to empty the drawers. There was so much in them that it would take some time to sort out the contents. With this job done she changed the bed linen, cleaned the windows, polished and hoovered. Amy looked round the bedroom. The carpet was new and a lovely shade of pink. Next week she would look round the shops for some pretty matching bed linen and curtains and matching wallpaper. She then went down to the kitchen and brought up her clothes and put them away.

By this time it was midday, so Amy stopped and got herself a sandwich and a drink and went and sat in the living room.

The cottage, although old, had been well kept. Her gran had put in central heating and double-glazing. The windows were mullioned, keeping the style of the cottage. The wiring had also been re-done. Amy decided that she would redecorate the cottage, and buy new carpets and some new furniture. The cottage was small but full of character. It consisted of old oak beams and nooks and crannies with a winding staircase that went up from a corner of the living room by the window. The living room boasted a bay window with a window seat and a stone fireplace with a gas fire fitted into the grate, which looked so real when it was lit, with real flames flickering over the coals.

The upstairs consisted of two bedrooms. Her gran's room was at the front, with a sloping ceiling and oak beams. The window looked out over the village street, across the school and on to the fields. The back bedroom was the same but a .little smaller, the window looking over the small back garden with a brick built shed in the corner. Years ago this had been the outside toilet.

Her gran had also had an extension to the cottage, and there was now a bathroom upstairs, next to the back bedroom, and one downstairs next to the kitchen. On the upstairs landing was a window with a deep recess. In this recess there was a bed, and when Amy had been a little girl she had always wanted to sleep in it. It was just the right size for a child.

Whilst Amy was eating her sandwiches she gazed happily about her. The sun was streaming through the bay window. It would soon be moving over the cottage and by the afternoon would be shining over the back garden and into the kitchen window.

As Amy was gazing round she noticed that there were photos of herself and her parents on the top of the television, which was in the corner between the window and the fireplace. As she did so she suddenly realised that there were no other photos anywhere in the cottage. Amy thought it strange that her gran did not have a photo of her late husband or her parents. There were no photos here, none at all. A shiver ran down Amy's spine as she suddenly realised that her gran had become a stranger – she knew nothing about her at all!

On impulse Amy rang her father. Henry and Penny had just got home and were happily looking at details of flights and costs to Australia.

"Hi, Dad," said Amy, "I was just thinking about gran, when I realised I don't know anything about her or her family, what can you tell me?"

"Well," Henry replied slowly, "I don't know much myself. I do know my father was called Henry and he was in the army. He was killed in the war before I was born. Whenever I asked her about my family she always said that everyone had been killed in the war."

"Where did she come from, Dad?"

"I've no idea, Amy, somewhere round here I expect."

"Oh, Dad, you're hopeless!"

"Your mother and I have been looking at holiday brochures, guess where we are going this summer?" teased Henry.

"I've no idea," she replied smiling.

"Australia!"

"To see Aunt Sheila?"

"Yes,"

"Oh, Dad, that's marvellous, when are you going?"

"During the school holidays – for six weeks," he replied happily.

"That's wonderful, I bet Mum is over the moon!"

"She certainly is!"

"I don't know," laughed Amy, "I'm not out of the house five minutes, and you two are planning things without me!"

They chatted for a few more minutes, and Amy rang off. She was pleased for her parents. It made her feel a bit less guilty about leaving home and inheriting so much money.

Amy spent the rest of the day cleaning the cottage and putting all her possessions away. By the end of the day everywhere looked spic and span. During the evening she got herself a meal in the small but well-fitted kitchen, and then sat in the living room and started making a list of the decorating she would like to do and the new things she would be able to buy with 'that cheque', which was burning a hole in her handbag.

Suddenly Amy heard a knock at the door. Puzzled she went to answer it, only to find an elderly man standing there. He was quite tall and sun-tanned with bright blue eyes and a mass of white hair.

"Good evening," he said politely, "you must be Amy?"

"That's right," she replied.

"My name is Charles Brown. I'm sorry to bother you, but I am an old friend of your grandmother's. I have just got back from my holiday and heard of her death. I would like to offer you my condolences."

"Thank you," replied Amy. He continued by asking her if she was selling the cottage.

"Oh, no, I am going to live here, I just moved in today." Charles Brown looked rather taken aback.

"I see," he said slowly.

"Why, did you want to buy it?" asked Amy.

"No, no, of course not, my dear." He looked extremely put out, and finally went away, wishing her a pleasant evening.

Amy was more puzzled than ever. She had never seen or heard of Mr Brown. How could he be a friend of her gran's without her knowing him? She ran over to the window and peeped round the curtains. She saw him leave the cottage, walk down to the road, and get into a blue car and drive away.

Amy was hurt and mystified. She and her gran had always been so close, and now she was becoming more of a mystery. Why had her gran never told her about her family. Who were her grandparents, and where had her gran come from? Who on earth was this Mr Brown, and why had her gran kept him a secret? Nothing made any sense.

Amy decided she would start tracing her ancestors. She knew she would not rest until she found out something about her gran's mysterious past. When she went back to work on Monday, she would ask if anyone knew how she could get started and what she had to do.

Amy's first night in her cottage was a restless one.

CHAPTER SIX
THE SEARCH BEGINS – MAY 1990

Amy spent the following day in the garden. It was a warm, sunny Sunday morning and the air was soft and warm. She felt her spirits lifting and her heart glow at the beauty of it all.

Dressed in some old clothes and trainers she stood and looked at the front garden, arms akimbo. What a mess! The grass was overgrown and dead daffodils and tulips were lying limp and bedraggled on the ground. She began by mowing the lawn and trimming the edges, which improved the garden straight away. Amy then set to and weeded the garden and cut down all the dead flowers and dug out the dead plants. She then hoed the garden, turning over the soil, the smell of the fresh earth invading her nostrils. Amy was interrupted all morning by friendly neighbours stopping for a chat and welcoming her to the village. She listened to the clip clop of the horseriders as they tapped their way along the road. When Amy had finished the front garden she was realised how hungry she was, so, locking the cottage, she nipped down to the Kings Head and sat in the bar, her trainers as muddy as the boots of some of the farmers who were sitting chatting, dogs at their feet. Amy bought herself a cheese and onion roll, and a half a cider, which she thoroughly enjoyed. The bar staff chatted to her and she felt she really belonged in this lovely village.

When she got back to the cottage Amy started on the back garden, which was quite private, and she was able to get on without much interruption. Annie, the next door neighbour had gone to visit her daughter, and the garden on the other side was completely hidden by a tall fence. Amy worked hard and breathed a sigh of relief when she had finished. The gardens were now neat and tidy, if not rather bare. She decided that as soon as her cheque was banked and cleared she would go to the local nursery and buy some new tools, a new electric mower and whole load of new plants.

By the end of the day Amy was happily tired. When she got upstairs she fell into bed, and was asleep the second her head touched the pillow.

The following day Amy drove off to work, still feeling a little stiff after her gardening session the day before! Her mind, now, was full of questions, and she was anxious to get 'that cheque' safely put away into the building society. She would then have to consider how she wanted the money invested. She decided to go to the building society in her lunch hour.

Amy got to work, locked her bag and coat in the cloakroom, went to the Chief Cashier for her 'float' and set up her till. Monday was always a busy day at the bank, but somehow, during the morning she managed to ask other members of staff if any of them knew how to trace their ancestors. Nobody seemed to have a clue, but then her friend, Gail, piped up, "Oh, Amy, I've just remembered, Joel Brent has been tracing his family tree, I'll bet he'll be able to help you." Somebody laughed.

"Trust Joel to do something boring like that!"

"Shut up, Pete," said Gail, "Joel may be boring compared to you lot, but he's a very nice man, and least he's got some manners!" There followed some banter that Amy ignored.

At the first possible chance Amy spoke to Joel about tracing her ancestors.

"No problem," he smiled. "We can have lunch together if you like, and I can tell you how to get started."

"Thanks, Joel."

"I'll meet you at the pub across the road at 12.30."

"I have to go to the building society first."

"OK, Amy, I'll get us a seat and wait for you."

Amy could hardly wait until lunch time. At 12.30. she dashed up to the building society, which was just up the High Street, to get the cheque safely put away. She prayed that no-one in the queue behind her would see it. The cheque was making her feel nervous and guilty. Whilst she stood in the queue she had a horrible feeling that Mr Brown (her strange visitor) was also in the queue, but dismissed it as fantasy.

Amy was glad to get to the pub, which was very popular at lunch times with it's tasty snacks and quick service. The pub had been modernised over the years. The carpet had given way to a wooden floor on which stood huge pots of plants. The seats were comfortable, set round heavy iron tables, and there were brass poles and white shaded lights dividing the pub into sections. When Amy walked in the pub was busy. There was much chatter and a haze of smoke floated over her head. She spotted Joel sitting in a corner, reading the Daily Telegraph. He smiled at her approach.

"I managed to get a quiet corner, so that we could talk in peace."

Amy smiled back, "You're very thoughtful." She sat down by Joel and they discussed what they would have for lunch. They agreed on chicken sandwiches and coffee, and Joel ordered for them both. Whilst they were waiting Amy told Joel her problem.

Joel began to explain the procedure of tracing ancestors.

"The first thing you will need," he began, "is your father's birth certificate. This will give you his date of birth and the place where he was born. You will also get his father's name and occupation, and his mother's name and maiden name. You will also get the address of his parents at the time of his registration.

With this information you can then get his parent's marriage certificate. As you will have both full names it won't be difficult. Once you have got this you will get the names and addresses of his parents, their ages, or full age if they are over 21. Their status, such as bachelor, spinster or widow comes next, followed by their occupations, and last of all both father's names and occupations – and don't forget the witnesses, they can sometimes be a valuable clue." Amy was fascinated.

"Once you have got the marriage certificate, you get their birth certificates. You will have the names of the fathers to give you a clue. You just go on then getting the next certificate in the chain. As registration did not start until July 1837, you will have to check the church registers for baptisms, marriages and burials, when you have got back that far."

Where will I get them from?" Amy asked eagerly.

"It depends where they were registered," he replied. "If they came from round here you could go to the local register office and order a copy. Births and deaths are simple enough, but if you want a marriage you will have to know which church where it took place as some towns have a lot of churches, and the staff won't always be prepared to check them all. The easier way would be to go to the local archives and check the registers yourself and get photocopies. The records are nearly all on microfiche, but they will have a photocopier. It would also be cheaper to get a photocopy, as they would cost you about 10p, where as an original copy would cost you £5.50."

"What if my family came from somewhere else?" she queried.

"Then you could go to the General Register Office in London. They have the registers of births, marriages and deaths for England and Wales. The registers are big heavy books, red for births, green for marriages and black for deaths. Each year is divided into four quarters, March, June, September and December, they are all set out in alphabetical order. All you get is a name, a registration district and a reference number, you will not get any more details until you have bought the actual certificate."

Amy was enthralled. Their food arrived, and she was able to think whilst they ate their sandwiches. The pub was now full and getting noisy.

"So," said Amy, raising her voice, "the first thing I will do this evening is go and see Dad, and get his birth certificate. I'll get a copy of it to keep."

"Good," replied Joel, "you can show it to me tomorrow, and I'll tell you what to do next. There are other ways of tracing your ancestors, but some of them have a 100 year rule."

"What does that mean?"

"Well," he continued," for example you can look at a census return, where you can get a whole family together, but you have to wait until 100 years have passed before you can see it."

"Wow!" exclaimed Amy, "that's a bit mean!"

"Tell me about it!" laughed Joel, who was eagerly waiting for the release of the 1891 census that would not be available until 1992. By this time Joel and Amy had to get back to the bank. They threaded their way through the busy pub, and carefully crossed the road, dodging the two-way traffic.

As Amy was driving home she suddenly realised that her gran must have had her birth and marriage certificate somewhere in the cottage. "I wonder why I haven't found them?" she thought to herself. After visiting her father she decided she would go through the cardboard box that was full of papers she had tipped out of the drawers. If they weren't there she would just have to look in every possible place she could find.

When Amy got home she rang her father, who agreed to look for his birth certificate. "I've got it somewhere," he had said on the phone.

After a quick tea Amy drove over to her parent's house. She let herself in and went into the living room. Her mother was out, but her father was sitting in his favourite armchair watching the news on the television. "Where's mum?" she asked.

"She's gone round to Molly's, next door, to tell them about our trip to Australia," he chuckled.

"She must be so excited," said Amy. "Dad, did you find it?" she asked impatiently.

"Yes, love, here you are." Henry handed her a small document covered in red writing. Amy opened it out, her face falling with disappointment.

"What's the matter, Amy?" asked Henry, looking up at her from his chair.

Oh, Dad," she cried. "I just can't believe it – this is a short birth certificate. It doesn't tell us anything about your parents. It's just got your name, date of birth and that you were born in Whitechapel in London."

"I'm sorry, Amy," frowned Henry, "but I don't have a full one." Amy smiled.

"Never mind, Dad, it can't be helped, but can't you tell me anything about gran at all?"

"I'm sorry, I can't. I didn't even know I'd been born in London." Henry had lived locally as long as he could remember, first at Bishops Fell, then here in Cropwell.

They chatted for a while, then Amy kissed her father goodbye, promising to return the certificate after she had copied it. She was keen to get back to the cottage and start searching.

As she drove home she did not notice that she was being followed.

As soon as Amy got home to Jade Cottage, she began to search through the contents in the cardboard box, very carefully,

41

but there were only old magazines, papers, receipts, and other useless pieces of paper. She then searched in the window seat, but it was full of books. Amy took out each one and shook them, but no pieces of paper fell out. She went through all the kitchen drawers and cupboards and all through the old sideboard in the living room, and even searched the airing cupboard, but there was nothing.

As a last resort Amy went up into the loft. She took a step ladder up on to the landing and climbed into the dark, forbidding opening. She switched on the light and started to climb through. The attic was hot and dusty. There was a lot of junk and bits and pieces that her gran no longer used, but didn't want to part with. Amy went through some old suitcases and boxes, but there were no documents of any kind.

By 11o'clock she gave up. She was getting more and more puzzled than ever by her gran's past. There wasn't as much as a photograph. There was simply – nothing!

Amy crawled out of the loft - she was filthy. Her clothes were covered in dust and cobwebs. She finally went downstairs and emptied the cardboard box, folded it flat, then put the box and all the contents into a black plastic bag and took them outside to put in the dustbin. As the bin was full, she dumped the bag of rubbish next to the bin. She then went back into the cottage, showered and washed her hair, letting out a squeal as she saw a spider being swept along past her wet feet, and get sucked into the plughole. She finally got to bed – tired and mystified.

Amy could hardly wait to see Joel the next day. When she finally managed to get hold of him she showed him her father's short birth certificate, which he let her photocopy in his office.

"Don't worry," he said kindly to Amy. "You have your father's full date of birth 1st March, 1942, and his place of birth, so it should be simple enough to get a full copy. If you give me your phone number, I will find out the address of the Whitechapel register office, and I will ring you this evening. All you have to do is write and ask for a full copy. Keep your letter short and to the point, enclose a stamped addressed envelope and a cheque for £5.50 made out to the Superintendent Registrar. You should get a reply within the week."

"Thanks, Joel, that's great," beamed Amy. Joel gave her his phone number in case she ever needed it.

Amy was late finishing work that day. She then got caught in heavy traffic going though Cropwell, and finally got stuck behind a huge tractor on the Cropwell Road. By the time she got home it was 6 o'clock.

She parked the car as usual at the side of the cottage. Her gran had stopped driving a few years ago. As there was no garage her gran had had a large car port put up along the side of the cottage, which had been a blessing, especially as on wet days Amy could leave the house and get straight into the car without getting wet! As Amy got out of the car she noticed that the black bag of rubbish she had put out the night before had gone. She frowned – the dustbin men were not due until Thursday, and this was Tuesday. She checked the bin – it was still full. Amy felt her heart miss a beat. She hurried into the cottage and locked the door.

Amy felt uneasy, who on earth would want a bag of old papers? It just seemed pointless. She took off her jacket and wandered round the cottage looking out of all the windows, to see if there was anyone lurking about, but there was no-one.

She eventually went into the kitchen to get herself something to eat. She put a jacket potato in the microwave and prepared some salad and cold meat, and made herself a drink. She then went into the living room and switched on the TV, the table lamp and the gas fire to make the room feel warm and cosy. She sat on the settee and had her meal, her eyes wandering to the window to see who was passing. Although Amy lived on the main road going through the village, her street only consisted of cottages, the village school, pub and church, so there wasn't much activity at that time of the evening.

She was still puzzling about the missing bag of rubbish when Joel rang to give her the address of the Whitechapel register office. She told him about the missing bag, but he was as puzzled as her. He did suggest that a tramp may have taken it, or a thief who just happened to be passing by.

When Joel rang off she sat and wrote out the letter asking for her father's full birth certificate. Perhaps, soon, she would be able to start unravelling her mystery.

Before going to bed Amy checked all the doors and windows to make sure they were locked.

Amy was scared.

CHAPTER SEVEN
PROBLEMS – MAY 1990

Amy went off to work again the next day. She was still feeling uneasy after the bag of old papers had gone missing. The papers were worthless that she had thrown out, who could possibly be interested in her gran's rubbish?

Amy was glad to be back at work, it did keep her troubled mind occupied. Joel met her again for lunch. He really was a nice man, she thought. He was not 'trendy' like most of the other young men at the bank, but he was clean and smart. He was quite tall with short dark hair, a rather swarthy skin and brown eyes that were serious behind gold rimmed glasses. Being such a serious person Amy found his rare smile breathtaking. She was getting to like Joel very much. He was just the kind of person Amy needed at a time like this.

After leaving work Amy called in at the supermarket to get some shopping. The store was busy and she had to push and shove with her trolley to get round the shelves, and then join a long queue to get served. She wheeled her trolley out to her car and put the shopping away. As she wheeled her trolley back to the store she looked up. Her heart missed a beat. Surely that was Mr Brown sitting in a blue car nearby. His tanned skin and white hair were quite noticeable. When she returned to her car she looked at him, but he had turned his head away. Perhaps it wasn't him at all. "I'm getting a nervous wreck!" she thought to herself.

Amy got home and parked her car near the door of the cottage as usual. She got her shopping out of the car and let herself in. She walked into the kitchen to put her shopping away. She stopped suddenly. There was something wrong, she knew. She looked round the kitchen and saw the corner of a tea-towel peeping out of one of the kitchen drawers that had not been shut properly. Now Amy was a very neat and tidy person like her father (her mother was just the opposite) and she knew that someone had been in her kitchen.

With her heart thumping Amy went across the stone flagged passage to the living room. Someone had been in here as well. Small items were in the wrong place, and the cushions of the settee had obviously been pulled out and not been put back properly. The cottage had been searched! Amy ran upstairs, and it was the same up there. Drawers had not been shut properly, and the carpet in the corner of her bedroom near the window was sticking up slightly. She went over and lifted the carpet to find a loose piece of floorboard. She lifted it up to find a little space underneath, an empty space.

Amy was horrified. Who on earth had been in her cottage and done such a thorough search? What on earth were they looking for? It suddenly dawned on her that it could have been the person who had stolen the bag of rubbish from outside. Were they looking for papers or documents? What secrets had her gran hidden in this cottage? She decided to ring the police. If the burglar was hanging about outside, the sight of the police might just frighten him away for good.

Amy ran down to the passage to telephone the police. She picked up the receiver to dial 999 when she realised that it was not exactly a dire emergency. She put down the receiver and decided to call the local police station. She didn't know the number! She picked up the telephone directory and with trembling fingers she riffled through the pages until she found it. She stood with shaking legs as the phone rang. A man's voice spoke.

"Cropwell police, how can I help you?"

"I...I've been burgled," stammered Amy. A kindly voice replied.

"Could you give me your name address please, Miss?"

"Y....yes it's Amy Kendal, I live at Jade Cottage in Bishop's Fell."

"What seems to be the problem, Miss?" Amy was starting to shiver.

"I've just come in from work, and someone has been in my home and searched it, and I'm scared..." she choked.

"Alright, Miss Kendal, now don't you worry, I'll get someone to come round. Just make sure you don't touch anything."

"Right, thank you...thank you...goodbye." Amy put down the receiver, then lifted it up again to ring her parents. She knew that they would both be home from work. Henry and Penny said they would come round immediately.

Whilst she waited for her parents Amy sat in the kitchen and tried to think. She was uneasy about telling them too much in case they should worry, so she decided not to tell them about the mysterious Mr Brown and the missing bag of rubbish. Amy was wondering whether it was Mr Brown who had broken into her cottage and stolen the bag of rubbish. He said he had been a friend of her gran's, if so he would probably know what she had got in the cottage, and was trying to steal it. Her mind was going round in circles at all the possibilities.

Henry and Penny arrived to see their daughter in a terrible state. Penny hugged Amy and asked, "Would you like to come home with us, dear?"

"No thanks, Mum, I'll be alright. I don't suppose they will come back now, and I'm waiting for the police."

"Is there anything missing, Amy?" asked Henry.

"I don't thinks so, Dad, I can't see anything obvious."

Penny bustled about the kitchen and started to make them all a cup of tea.

"The police told me to touch nothing, Mum," said Amy nervously.

"Maybe, but that will not stop me making us all a cup of tea," retorted Penny.

Whilst they were drinking their tea, the police arrived. When Amy answered the door she saw two plain clothes men. A tall grey-haired one and a short fair-haired one. As Amy let them in, the taller one spoke to her.

"Miss Kendal?"

"Yes."

"I am Detective Sergeant Allen, and this is Detective Constable Hawker." Det. Con. Hawker was carrying bag.

"Good evening, Miss." He smiled politely. Sergeant Allen spoke to her again.

"Would you like to show us where you were broken in?"

47

"Broken in?" exclaimed Amy frowning. "I...I don't know."

"Well," he replied raising his eyebrows, "your burglar must have got in somewhere."

"I...I'm sorry," stammered Amy, "I just didn't notice."

"Let us have a look then, shall we?"

Amy felt such a fool! With blushing cheeks she showed the two detectives round the cottage so that they could check all the windows, but none of them were broken or damaged. They went back to the door to check the lock, but that wasn't damaged either.

"Does anyone have a key to your cottage, Miss Kendal?" asked the taller detective.

"A key!" gasped Amy. "Only my parents have a spare key. I used it when I first moved into the cottage, and then gave it back to them. I'm sure no-one else has a key."

"Well," he answered frowning, "Someone has used a key, probably a skeleton key."

Amy was horrified to think that her burglar had had a key! Sergeant Allen suggested that she got her lock changed as soon as possible, get a chain put on the door and put in an alarm.

The two detectives asked her if there was anything missing, but she had to tell them she wasn't sure. Her TV and video were still there, and so were all other big items. She told them that the cottage appeared to have just been searched, and showed them the corner of her bedroom where the carpet had been lifted.

"Do you keep any money in the house, Miss Kendal?"

"No," she replied, "I only have what's in my purse."

"I think you'll find that your burglar was just after money, Miss Kendal, we'll just take some fingerprints to see if we can find any of anyone on record, that's about all we can do for now. Perhaps later in the week you can let us know if there is anything missing." Amy agreed.

The two detectives fingerprinted the door handles and the drawers and took photographs. When they left they gave Amy a leaflet on security measures, and told her to ring them straight away if she had any more problems.

When they had gone Amy sighed with relief. She looked at her father. "Dad, could you get the lock changed for me, do you think?"

"No problem," replied Henry firmly. Henry knew half the population of Cropwell. Although there was more than one junior school in Cropwell, Henry had taught a lot of the children of the local tradesmen. They all knew him and liked him. He would ring round and make the arrangements for her.

This decided, the three of them set to and cleaned up the messy grey fingerprint powder, and put Amy's shopping away. Henry insisted that he and Penny take Amy over to the Kings Head for a meal. They locked up the cottage and walked along the village to the pub. The landlord recognised them straight away.

They found a seat near the large fireplace. The fire was warm and welcoming as the evening had gone chilly. Henry went up to the bar to get them all a drink, and chat to the landlord. He came back to the table with the menu. There were quite a few people in the pub all talking quietly, and music was being softly played, it was all very relaxing. Henry and Amy decided on a peppered steak and chips and Penny had a salad. She was very conscious of the weight she had been putting on over the years, and was on another one of her diets!

After a very pleasant evening Henry and Penny walked Amy home, making sure all was safe before leaving her alone. When they had gone Amy rang Joel. She apologised for the lateness of the hour, but she felt that he was the only person she could talk to about her mystery. They both agreed that Mr Brown was the most likely suspect. He was obviously following Amy about, and could have got into her cottage during the day when he knew she would be at work. He obviously wanted something that belonged to her grandmother. Had he found it? She had no idea what it could have been. Joel was very comforting on the phone, and she began to feel calmer.

Amy had another restless night.

Amy had a trying week. She was nervous about the burglary, although she was sure that nothing she owned had been taken.

She was anxious about the reply from the Whitechapel register office. What was she going to find on her father's birth certificate? Perhaps her grandmother hadn't lost a husband. What if she had run away from him years ago, and he had turned up at the cottage looking for her? Was that why she had had her heart attack? Perhaps she had never been married and didn't want people to know? The possibilities were endless!

Amy had a reply from the Whitechapel register office on the Friday. She was thrilled to get a reply so soon, but she received another shock when she received a letter to say that they had no record of her father's birth, and were returning her cheque. Amy could have wept with disappointment. It was suddenly as though her family didn't exist. She began to wonder whether her father's short birth certificate was somebody else's or maybe it was a forgery, but dismissed this as impossible.

Amy had to work on the Saturday morning, and as Joel was also there she was able to show him the letter. His only suggestion to comfort Amy was to say that his birth certificate must have been lost during the war.

They finished work at lunchtime so Joel and Amy went for as drink together at the pub across the road, the 'Black Horse.' Joel could see that Amy was upset. He took her hand in his firm, strong one, and looked into her sad eyes.

"Can you afford to pay a researcher?" he asked gently. Amy felt uncomfortable, as Joel did not know about 'that cheque'.

"Yes, of course," she replied.

"Well, I suggest that you pay a researcher to check the baptisms of all the churches in Whitechapel, to see if your father can be found there."

That's sounds a good idea, I'll do that," she replied brightening up. She ran her fingers through her hair and pushed in behind her ears. The pub was full and noisy and hot.

"I'll find one for you and let you know."

"Thanks, Joel, and thanks for all your help." Joel and Amy finished their drinks and pushed their way through the crowded pub. Joel went home to change and go for a game of squash with some friends, and Amy had a wander round the town looking at furniture and carpets and wallpaper, to get some ideas for when she redecorated the cottage.

During the weekend Joel rang Amy with the address of researcher who had been recommended to him by a member of his local family history society. She wrote off a letter to him, and wondered how long she would have to wait before she ever solved this mystery.

CHAPTER EIGHT
A WAITING GAME – JUNE/JULY 1990

By the beginning of June Amy's cottage boasted a brand new alarm system, a new lock, a chain and two stout bolts on the inside of the door. She felt much safer, but was still troubled by her gran's mysterious past.

Amy hadn't planned a holiday this year. She usually went away with her friend, Kay, but she had got married in the March, just before her gran Kendal had died. Kay and her new husband had gone to live in Stratford-on-Avon, and although she and Amy kept in touch they hadn't visited each other, and Kay would now be taking her holidays with her husband.

Amy decided she would take two weeks off in July whilst her parents were away in Australia, and have the cottage decorated. The outside of the cottage was looking lovely now, with neat lawns and flowerbeds blazing with colour. As the days were drawing out Amy spent many evenings in the garden, often chatting to the neighbours who had known her since she was a little girl. She had also bought some expensive garden furniture, a lovely green wrought iron table and chairs, a garden swing with a canopy and a matching sun-lounger and a barbecue. She was planning to have some friends round one weekend, for a meal.

Henry had found a painter and decorator for her and he had been round and measured up, and given her an estimate for the re-decorating of the two bedrooms, the landing and stairs and the living room. He had also told Amy how much paper she needed for each room, and agreed to come and start work in the middle of July, the start of Amy's holiday.

Amy's kitchen and two bathrooms did not re-decorating. When her gran had last had them done she had let Amy choose the tiles and units and decor. All she needed was some new pretty towels for the bathrooms, and perhaps some new crockery and matching kitchen ware. "Dear Gran," Amy thought sadly, twisting her soft hair with her fingers, "Why did she love me so much? She must have always planned to leave me this cottage. Everything she bought for it was what I liked."

During the next few weeks Amy spent her weekends shopping. She was so worried about anyone finding out about her new found wealth she was forced to do her shopping alone. She chose pretty, matching bed linen, wallpaper and lampshades for her bedroom, in shades of pink to match the carpet. The duvet cover and pillowcases were edged in frills and lace. She chose similar ones for the spare bedroom in shades of soft blues and greens.

For the living room she chose a very expensive cream leather suite. She picked two two-seater settees, as the room was not big enough for a large three-piece suite. She chose curtains and carpets in warm autumn shades and a nest of tables in a dark oak to match the beams. She also bought a couple of lovely oil paintings, scenic ones with little girls in long dresses. She also treated herself to some large plants in heavy pots and vases of silk flowers.

Amy had a wonderful time shopping for her cottage. She still couldn't believe that she had so much money to spend. Her new happiness was only spoilt by that wretched Mr Brown. Amy was convinced that he was still following her about. What on earth for she could not imagine. She could only guess that whatever he was looking for he had not found, but why follow her? What if she had found something, how would he know anyway? The only person she could confide in was Joel. He would listen to her worries and calm her down. Amy did not tell any of her friends at work, as they would probably laugh, and the lads would tease her endlessly. At least Joel believed her and cared about her.

The weather was getting warmer now and Amy started going out more. She went out with the girls from work some evenings to discos and to the pictures and for Chinese meals. She had a couple of dates with Joel, too, and one Sunday he took her over to Coventry to meet his family

Joel's parents lived in a large detached house on the lovely tree-lined Kenilworth Road on the outskirts of Coventry, not far from the railway station, and near to the Memorial Park, which seemed to stretch for miles. Joel's father was a bank manager in Coventry. His name was Freeman, which was a family name, appearing many times on Joel's family tree. Freeman was a tall, heavily built man, with dark brown hair and brown eyes. Amy thought he looked more like a rugger player than a bank manager! Joel's mother, Maria, was lovely. She was Italian, small, excitable, and funny. She had long black hair, merry brown eyes, and a wide smiling mouth, and Amy liked her instantly. Joel also had a brother, James and a sister Sofia, who were both older than Joel and had young children. They all lived in London. They were a charming family and made Amy feel welcome.

Maria's parents, who still lived in Italy, were growing old. Maria was the youngest of a large family and the only one who had left the country. Every year, at the end of June, Joel and his parents would go over to Italy for a holiday to visit their family. Joel had many cousins over there and always enjoyed himself immensely.

By the middle of July Henry and Penny were off to Australia. Amy had helped Penny with her last minute shopping, Penny was so excited about their trip, and was getting herself into such a 'tizz' that Henry and Amy couldn't help but laugh at her. Amy helped her mother clean up the house and leave everywhere nice for their return. Henry's next-door neighbours, Molly and Richard, were going to keep an eye on the house for them whilst they were away.

Her parent's flight to Australia was from Heathrow. They had friends, who taught at the same school as Henry, who were going to take them to the airport, and pick them up on their return. As they were flying on the Monday afternoon, Amy popped round to say goodbye to them before she went to work. She was glad her parents were having this lovely holiday. Next year she would have an exotic holiday, perhaps with Joel?

After her parents had gone Amy had a letter from the researcher in London. She was bitterly disappointed with the result. The researcher told her that he had searched every church register in the Whitechapel area for a Henry Kendal with a mother, Caroline, but there was none. He had found one possible Henry Kendal baptised, but he had died at the age of 6 months. He did remind her that many documents were destroyed during the war. He did apologise for not being able to help her, and enclosed a bill that she paid.

Amy's heart sank. The mystery was getting deeper. She had no idea what to do next or where to look. What was she going to say to her father? Fortunately he was now in Australia and by the time he got back he would hopefully have forgotten that she was tracing his family tree.

Amy decided that for now she would just have to leave her mystery unsolved.

Little did she know that the terrible truth was not far away.

CHAPTER NINE
A SHOCK FOR AMY – AUGUST 1990

It was a glorious Sunday morning in the middle of August. Amy woke up to find the sun streaming through her bedroom window like spears of gold. She lay there amongst the frills and lace of her new bed linen, feeling content and happy, and thinking about the lovely day she had had on the Saturday. The cottage was now finished and looked simply beautiful, and she had been ready to entertain friends. The day before, Saturday, she had hurriedly cleaned the cottage, and then gone to the supermarket to get food and drink for the barbecue she was having later in the day. Joel had come round and the two of them had set out her new garden furniture and prepared all the food for the barbecue. In the afternoon her guests arrived, Gail from the bank and her boyfriend, and Neil, Joel's friend who was on leave from the Royal Navy and his current girlfriend. They had all sat in the back garden, lazing in the sunshine and drinking the punch that she had made. They had all talked and laughed. Everyone had loved Amy's cottage, and envied her lovely home and her independence.

During the evening they had all tucked into the delicious food that consisted of steak, chicken legs, kebabs and beefburgers that they had with salad and thick crusty rolls, dripping with butter. The girls had wine to drink and the men had cans of beer. They had such a lovely evening, and sat out in the garden until late. The night was still and warm with the smell of the honeysuckle, which grew along the high fence, invading the air. The men talked quietly and the girls had giggled. When everyone had finally gone, Joel helped Amy clear away, and after kissing her goodnight, he caught a taxi home. Joel was playing squash with Neil on Sunday morning, and then he was going to return to the cottage, where he and Amy would have a quiet barbecue to themselves.

Amy stretched and smiled to herself, and reluctantly eased herself out of bed. She got up and went to the window, and drew back the curtains. She looked out over the village school, which was bathed in sunshine, and to the fields beyond where lazy cows were grazing, instead of the usual sheep and lambs, which were always there in the spring.

She sighed happily, running her slim fingers through her soft tousled hair, and made her plans for the day. She would have breakfast, then spend a couple of hours tidying the garden. She would have liked to have done it on the Saturday, but didn't have time. When she had finished the garden she would have a sunbathe in the back garden, and then, later, would prepare the barbecue and wait for Joel.

After breakfast Amy put on some old shorts and a T-shirt and her old trainers, and set about the front garden. She mowed and trimmed the lawn and weeded the garden. As usual she was stopped by friendly neighbours taking their dogs for a walk. Amy would sit on the low stone wall at the front of the garden whilst she chatted. The usual horseriders trotted along the road for their Sunday outing, and tractors slowly grumbled their way along the road, getting in everyone's way. Amy was thrilled with her garden, and thought how pleased her gran would be if she knew.

When Amy had finished the front garden, she took the lawn mower and her tools through to the back garden, shutting the tall gate behind her. It was peaceful in the back garden, as Annie always went to her daughter's on a Sunday, and her neighbours on the other side were away on holiday. The back garden now boasted a circular lawn trimmed with flowers, with a large flowerbed under the kitchen window. Amy mowed and trimmed the lawn, and put the mower back into the shed, which just left her a bit of weeding to do. Amy had almost finished weeding when she had trouble with the flowerbed under the window. She came across the biggest dandelion she had ever seen. She dug down as far as she could with the trowel, but it wouldn't budge, the roots were much too deep. With a 'tut' of annoyance she marched to the shed to fetch the garden fork to try and dig it out.

Amy pushed the fork into the ground as far as she could to get at the stubborn roots. As she did so the prongs of the fork hit something hard. Amy poked about with the fork to see what was in the way, when she saw something that looked like a metal box. Puzzled she started to dig round it. The ground was quite hard, and she finally had to get down on her hands and knees, and using the trowel she managed to clear some of the soil away. She looked down and frowned – it was a metal box – like a big black cash box with a handle on top. What on earth was it doing there? She realised with a shock, that it must have belonged to her grandmother, as her gran had lived in the cottage for over forty years.

Amy dug and pulled and scrabbled to release the box. She was hot, sweating and breathless, and her neatly manicured nails were soon filled with dirt. Amy eventually dragged the box out of the hole, and laid it on the grass. "God!" thought Amy, "that nearly gave me a heart attack."

Amy's blood suddenly ran cold. A heart attack – of course! Maybe this is what had killed her grandmother. She must have come out here on that wet April day and buried this box. But why? It must have been something very important to her, which she wanted no one to see. Amy examined the box. Her mind was racing with all the possibilities. She tried to open it, but it was locked. "Damn!" she exclaimed, under her breath. She struggled and pulled at the handle, but it wouldn't budge. She sat back, red-faced and panting. She then started to panic – what if this was what Mr, Brown was after? She looked round her nervously – she mustn't let him know she had found it!

Amy pushed the box out of sight amongst the flowers. Her mind working fast, she pushed the soil back into the hole, and tidied the mess. She grabbed the fork and ran to the shed. Her heart was pounding as she left the fork against the shed wall, and rummaged through her gran's old toolbox for a screwdriver. She found a big one at last! Amy ran over to the flowerbed, snatched up the box and ran into the cottage, locking the door behind her.

Amy put the box on the kitchen table, and stared at it. She was shaking with excitement, her eyes alight, her flushed cheeks smeared with dirt, her hair a mess. She didn't notice how filthy she was as she pushed the screw driver under the lid of the box, twisting and turning until it finally opened. Amy looked into the box, breathless with anticipation. Inside were some old brown envelopes wrapped in a polythene bag. She went to take them out of the bag, when she realised her hands were filthy. With a curse she ran to the downstairs bathroom and scrubbed her hands and nails. She didn't notice the dirt on her face and arms and her legs and clothes – she was too excited!

Amy went back into the kitchen. She sat at the table, taking a deep breath to calm her down. With shaking fingers she took out the polythene bag and eased out the brown envelopes.

She peeped into the first one, and gasped. Photographs! She took them out carefully. They were old black and white photos of people...who were they? She peeped into the other envelopes slowly...there were newspaper cuttings, letters and documents. Amy was thrilled. The letters were addresses to Mrs C. Kendal, so they must have belonged to her grandmother! But why did she bury them? Amy soon found out. Her pleasure turned to shock when she saw that the documents and papers were all written in German!

Amy sat stunned. She could not believe her eyes. Her gran must have been a German – no wonder she had not been able to find anything out. What was she going to do now? She couldn't speak a word of German. She must ring Joel.

Amy dashed into the passage and rang Joel. His rich, deep voice answered the phone. "Joel!" she babbled, "I've found a box buried in the garden, and it's full of documents and photos!"

"Amy, that's wonderful!" he replied.

"But, Joel, they are all in German!" There was a silence.

"Are you sure?" he asked quietly.

"Well, it looks like German to me," she replied, starting to panic.

"Amy, calm down!"

"But, Joel, what am I going to do?" she squeaked.

"Amy, I learned German at school, and I still have my German dictionary, I'll come straight round," Joel replied, trying to sound calm.

"Oh, Joel, that's wonderful, but be careful in case that Mr Brown is hanging around. I'm sure that this box is what he's been looking for."

"I'll be careful, don't worry. I'll be with you in about twenty minutes." Joel put down the phone. He was worried. If Amy's gran was born in Germany, and hadn't wanted anyone to know, it looked bad.. He walked swiftly into his living room, found the dictionary and a magnifying glass (a must for family historians) and shoved them into a Sainsbury's carrier bag, along with a bottle of wine he had bought for their barbecue. He picked up his keys, locked his door and ran down to his car. He then drove off to the nearest garage and bought some flowers for Amy. He wanted his visit to look normal in case Mr Brown was watching.

Whilst Joel was on his way, Amy went back to the kitchen to her 'find'. As she couldn't read the documents she put them all back in their envelopes and started looking at the photos. The first one was of a little girl of about 5 years of age, with fair curly hair and a shy smile. "Why, that's me!" thought Amy, but when she turned it over it had 'Fransiska meine liebe tochter' written on the back. The next photo was of a small boy, also with fair hair, dressed in baby clothes. On the back was written 'Heinrich' Amy's eyes lit up at the sight of the next photo. It was of a fair-haired young woman wearing a silky suit and a big hat, standing beside a handsome man in army uniform. It looked like a wedding photo. She turned it over and on the back was written 'unsere hochzeit tag'. What on earth did it mean? Amy was frustrated at not knowing what the words meant.

The next photo was of a young woman with long fair hair. She was wearing a long dress and was laughing. On the back was written 'Lilli meine fraundliche schlester.' This lovely girl was in the next photo, possibly another wedding photo, with the girl wearing a beautiful silky dress and coat and a wide-brimmed hat. She was standing with a man in uniform, too. On the back of the photo was written 'Lilli und Hans'. The last photo was of an elderly couple standing in front of a lovely house. On the back was written 'meine eltern'.

Amy was enthralled with the old photographs. Who on earth were these people? Amy sat and gazed at them. The men were obviously soldiers and looked so smart in their uniforms. She was still gazing at the photographs, when there was a knock at the door. Amy nearly jumped out of her skin. She ran to the door, "Who is it?" she cried.

"It's me," called out Joel.

"Thank goodness you're here!" exclaimed Amy opening the door. She almost dragged Joel into the passage. He gave her the flowers and the wine as they moved into the kitchen.

"Joel, how lovely, thank you!" Amy put the wine in to the fridge and the flowers into the sink. She grabbed Joel's arm. "Come and see," she cried, and dragged him over to the table, and they both sat down. Joel took the dictionary and the magnifying glass out of the bag.

"Right," said Joel. "Let's see what you've got." Amy pulled her chair up close to Joel, and showed him the first photograph of the little girl.

"I thought she was me at first," she explained to Joel. He turned the photograph over. "What does it say?" she asked eagerly.

"It says, 'Fransiska, my lovely daughter.'" he said slowly.

"Daughter! but whose?" exclaimed Amy. She passed Joel the photo of Heinrich and then the photograph of the first young couple. He looked at it and frowned.

"What's up?" she asked.

"This uniform – if you look carefully – is a German uniform."

Amy's face paled. "Oh, no!" she whispered. Joel turned over the photograph and studied the writing.

"This says 'our wedding day' but whose I wonder?" Joel, still frowning picked up the photograph of the blonde girl. He looked at the back. "This one's easy, it says 'Lilli, my dear sister,'" said Joel, "and this is probably a wedding photo – Lilli and Hans. Look, Amy, this is a German uniform, too." Joel was becoming uneasy. If these people were Amy's family then her ancestors were Nazis. The last photograph with the old couple was translated as 'my parents'.

"Well!" exclaimed Joel, "What a find!" What else have you got there?" Amy tipped out carefully the contents of the next envelope. On the top was a list. Heads together they stared at it.

Einteilen

Der Artz

Peter Michaels

Harley Street, London.

Gasthaus besitzer

Theodore Schen

Golden Lion,

Lime Street
Whitechapel
London.

Der Kempelbehindler
Harold Steel
High Street,
Cropwell.

Der Anwahlt
James Harrison
24 High Street,
Cropwell.

Der Lehrer
Gerald Smith
Bishops Fell.

"What does is mean, Joel?" whispered Amy.

"I'll need the dictionary," said Joel quietly. He opened it and started searching. "Well, *einteilen* means 'contacts'...*der arzt* means 'doctor' – pretty obvious being in Harley Street. The next one is obviously an inkeeper. *Der kempelbehindler*...I don't know this one." He turned the pages of the dictionary and frowned. "It's antique dealer," he said puzzled. "*Der anwahlt* is a solicitor...and I know that *der lehrer* is a schoolteacher."

They both sat silent for a moment.

"What do you think, Joel?" asked Amy, her face puzzled.

Joel looked hesitant.

"I don't think you will like what I think!" he replied softly.

"Tell me," she begged.

"Well, I think these photos are of your family, and I think your gran came over to England for some reason, and this," he pointed to the list, "is her list of contacts. I think she must have arrived in London and then moved up to Bishops Fell, to be a schoolteacher, and she stayed here. The people on the list are all the people she might need for help, but I don't know why she would want an antiques dealer." Joel did not want Amy to know how worried he was becoming, and that the actual list was either of German spies or English traitors, most of them being in this area.

"What else is there?" he asked Amy. She passed a couple of newspaper cuttings that were yellow with age. Joel picked them up and looked at the first one carefully. He frowned and his brown eyes widened as he looked at the two men in uniform, in the picture.

"What is it?" Amy grasped his arm.

"This man on the left is the man in your first photo. His name is Heinrich Koner, and I think it says that he has been killed. The man next to him is Adolf Hitler."

"Oh, no!" gasped Amy. "You think my gran's family were Nazis?"

"It looks like it," he replied cautiously.

"Joel, this is awful – no wonder my gran hid all this away." They looked at the next cutting – it showed Adolf Hitler again, but this time with a beautiful woman. It appeared that she was the widow of Heinrich Koner, and her name was Christina."

"I'll need the dictionary for the rest of this article," said Joel. He ran his strong fingers through his dark hair, and took a deep breath. "Anything else?" he asked, his eyes serious. Amy picked up the next faded brown envelope and peeped inside, and took out the letters. There were four of them, all addressed to Mrs C. Kendal, Jade Cottage, Bishops Fell. Amy and Joel stared at them.

"Amy," said Joel, "there are no stamps on these letters, they must have been delivered by hand."

"Of course," Amy murmured breathlessly. She opened the first letter. On the top was an address in Berlin and a date – 1942 or 1943. The letter was addressed to Christina. Amy and Joel looked at each other in amazement. Amy's grandmother was Christina Koner! They looked at the end of the letter – it had been sent by Lilli, her sister. They quickly opened the other letters, and they were all the same – to Christina from Lilli.

"I can't believe it," whispered Amy in a shocked voice.

"Pass me those photos, Amy, let's see if we can work out this family." She passed the photographs to Joel, who studied them carefully. Eventually he spoke. "Right, let's say that your gran was Christina. She married Heinrich Koner. Her sister was Lilli, and her husband was Hans. That leaves the two children, Fransiska and Heinrich." He looked at Amy. "I think they were your gran's children." he said softly.

"But what happened to them?" asked Amy frowning.

"Well, I don't know about Fransiska, but Heinrich is the German for Henry." The penny suddenly dropped.

"My dad, oh my God, my dad!" cried Amy. Joel tried to calm her down.

"We might be wrong, Amy."

"No, Joel, I think you're right. That's why I can't find his birth certificate, he was born in Germany - the son of a Nazi! God, I need a drink!"

"So do I!" replied Joel, rubbing a hand over the back of his neck. Amy went over to the fridge to fetch the bottle of wine Joel had brought. With shaking hands she poured them both a glass. Joel could have done with something a bit stronger!

Joel got out his cigarettes and lit up, taking a deep breath. Amy passed him an ashtray. "Could I have one please, Joel?" she asked.

"Of course, I didn't know you smoked."

"I don't usually, but right now I need something to calm me down."

They sat in silence for some time smoking and sipping their wine, both trying to digest all they had found.

"I wonder why my gran came to England with my dad, and left all her family behind?" queried Amy.

"Perhaps her family were all killed, and she came here for safety," suggested Joel.

"Yes, but if she was a friend of the Nazis, she could have come here as a spy," said Amy amazed.

"I think I had better start translating these letters," replied Joel," they may give us some answers." Amy agreed.

The time seemed to have flown by. "Amy," suggested Joel, "whilst I try and translate these letters, why don't you get us something to eat?"

"Of course, I'd forgotten we were having a barbecue!" Glad of something to do whilst her head was reeling from the shock, Amy prepared some salad, and put a couple of steaks under the grill, and cut up some crusty bread and buttered it. By the time the meal was ready Joel had got the gist of the letters which were quite short.

Whilst they were eating Joel told Amy the brief contents of the letters.

"It seems that your gran came to England with your dad as a baby – I don't know why. She left her little daughter, Fransiska, in Germany with her sister Lilli and her husband, Hans. I can only assume she left Fransiska in Germany as she would have given the game away, not speaking English. Lilli writes to say that all is well, and Fransiska sends her love. She also asks about Heinrich. The rest is general chit-chat, but the last letter, in September 1943, Lilli says that they fear that Germany is going to lose the war, and they are going to America with friends. Lilli promises your gran that when they arrive in America, she will send her the address so that she and Heinrich can join them. I can only guess that Lilli and her family were killed, so your gran was left here, and decided to stay."

Amy's eyes filled with tears. "Poor, Gran, she must have been heartbroken at losing her little girl." She picked up the photo of Fransiska and gazed at it. "I thought this photo was of me - I must look like Fransiska – now I know why my gran loved me so much, I reminded her of her of her little daughter."

Amy cleared away the plates from the table. She was very quiet, and trying not to cry. She slowly returned to the table and sat down.

"Are you OK Amy?" asked Joel kindly. She nodded. Joel passed her a cigarette and poured her some more wine.

"I...I'm fine...really. What else have we got?"

"Two more envelopes, Amy," replied Joel, taking them out of the box. One of them was quite heavy. He tipped up the envelope and some small, heavy objects fell out – all wrapped in soft, little fabric envelopes. Joel opened one and out fell a gold coin. On the front of it was the head of Adolf Hitler. Joel and Amy looked at each other in astonishment.

"My God!" exclaimed Joel, "just look at this, I've never seen anything like it!"

"It must be very rare," whispered Amy.

"Yes," returned Joel, "and worth a bomb!" They suddenly looked at each other. "The antiques dealer!" they both cried together.

"Of, course," breathed Amy, "She's been selling these over the years, that's where her money's come from!" Amy looked hard at Joel, "Do you think they were stolen?"

"I've no idea, Amy, but we could go to the library and look at their books on foreign coins, and see if we can find anything."

"How many are there?" asked Amy, starting to pick them up. There were eight. "I can't believe all this," said Amy bewildered. "I feel as though I am in a dream."

"Right," said Joel firmly, "let's get the last envelope over with." Joel took out some faded sheets of paper with typing on them, they were some sort of documents.

"What are they?" whispered Amy puzzled. Joel studied them, and then checked the dictionary.

"They are certificates," he replied," but they are nothing like ours."

Amy grabbed his arm, "What do they say?" They both looked closely at the first one. Joel began to translate slowly.

"This says *Geburtsurkunde*...birth certificate...born in *Tiergarten*, Berlin...Fransiska Koner...born...10 September 1938. *Burggrafenstrasse* 31...that's the address...*vater*...that's father...Heinrich Koner...oberst....I think that means Colonel...of 0 Panzer Regiment...*evanelisch*. Let me see...that means protestant...*wohnhaft*...resident...in *Burggrafenstrasse* 31, *Tiergarten*. *Mutter*...that's mother... she is Christina Koner...*geborene*, that's her maiden name, Colberg.

"...*wohnhaft bei ihrem ehemann*.....residing with her husband. Now down here we have Berlin...*Tiergarten ben* 20, September...1938. That must be the date she was registered, and look at this, Amy there is a stamp with the Prussian eagle with a swastika in it's tail!"

"Wow!" gasped Amy, just look at that! It's Fransiska's birth certificate...and your right, they are nothing like ours at all, it's even got the father's religion. What else is there?"

Heads together they peered at the rest of the certificates.

The next one was the birth certificate of Amy's grandmother. Joel's finger moved slowly along the document.

"Here we go, Christina Colberg...born...*Tiergarten*...7th February 1917...*Flensburgerstrasse* 25.....father...Franz Colberg ...*der lehrer*...schoolteacher...*avenglisch*...same address...and mother...Lilli Colberg...nee Badel... The next certificate is a marriage....Heirich Koner to Christina Colberg 4th April,1937...looks like the register office...*Tiergarten*...and it gives both parents names, look...Gunther Koner and Amelia Richter and Franz Colberg and Lilli Badel...and here's the witnesses...Hans and Lilli Muller...your gran's sister and her husband."

Amy sat enthralled as she listened to the names of her ancestors, her hands were clasped together, and her eyes were shining with excitement. Joel moved on to the next certificate and frowned.

"That's funny," he mumbled, running his knuckles gently over his mouth.

"What's wrong, Joel?" Amy asked anxiously.

"Well, according to this death certificate Heinrich Koner, Panzer Regiment...was killed in 1940, and attached to it is a letter which looks like a letter to Christina informing her of his death on the battlefield."

"1940!" squeaked Amy. "Then who was the father of Dad?" Joel turned to the last certificate.

"Here we are...Heinrich Koner born 1st March 1942, same address as Fransiska...I can't read the father...it looks as though someone has tried to rub it out. The mother is still Christina Koner nee Colberg." He picked up the magnifying glass and they both stared at the certificate, Joel moving the glass slowly over the father's name, suddenly gasped with shock. Amy snatched the magnifying glass off Joel and pulled the certificate towards

Geburtsurkunde

(Standesamt Berlin - Tiergarten   Nr. 3146/38   )

Fransiska Koner

ist am 10 September 1938

in Berlin , Burggrafenstrasse31, ————————————— geboren.

Vater: Heinrich Köner, Oberst Panzer Regiment 10 avengelisch
wohnhafte Burggrafenstrasse 31 Tiergarten.

Mutter: Christina Köner geborene Colberg, wohnhaft
bei ihrem Ehemann.

Änderungen der Eintragung:

Berlin   - Tiergarten   , den 20. September   19.38

Der Standesbeamte

In Vertretung:

Geburtsurkunde

(Standesamt Berlin — Tiergarten   Nr. 4103/17)

—— Christina Colberg ——

ist am 7. Februar 1917

in Berlin Flensburgerstrasse 25 ———— geboren.

Vater: Franz Colberg Lehrer avengelisch
wohnhaft Flensburgerstrasse 25 Tiergarten

Mutter: Lilli Colberg geborene Badel
wohnhaft bei ihrem ehemann

Änderungen der Eintragung:

Berlin — Tiergarten ——, den 15. Februar 19 17

Der Standesbeamte

In Vertretung:

Stand B 27
Mat. 2843 ● Din B 4 50 000 8. 41

Geburtsurkunde

(Standesamt Berlin : – Tiergarten   Nr. 1483/42)

_____ Heinrich Koner _____

ist am   1 März 1942

in Berlin , Burggrafenstrasse 21, _____
_____ geboren.

Vater: *Karl Koner* _____ avengelisch

wohnhaft _ _ _   Tiergarten.

Mutter: Christina Koner geborene Colberg wohnhaft
Burggrafenstrasse 31

Änderungen der Eintragung:

_____

_____

Berlin   – Tiergarten _____ , den   10 März   19 42

Der Standesbeamte

In Vertretung: _____

her. She looked through it carefully and her face drained of colour...she looked at Joel, whose face was pale... Amy's father was the illegitimate son of Adolf Hitler!

Amy felt sick.

"No. No. No!" she cried. "It can't be true!" She was now trembling with shock. Her dear father was the son of Adolf Hitler. She buried her head in her hands and shook. This was a nightmare! Joel went off to the living room and came back with a glass of brandy. He put an arm round her shoulders.

"Amy, drink this!" He put the glass to her white lips, and made her drink slowly until the colour came back into her cheeks. Her bare, muddy legs were shivering. The whole room seemed to have gone cold, even the sun had dipped behind the trees, as if hiding away in shame. Joel lit them both a cigarette, then put his arm round Amy again, rubbing her shaking arm. She took the cigarette gratefully.

"We could be wrong, Amy," he said quietly.

"No," she answered softly. My gran killed herself burying that box in the garden. She was desperate for no-one to find it, and I think that Mr Brown is after this box – he either wants to blackmail me or he wants those coins." Joel had to agree.

"Amy," went on Joel, "all this you have found is dynamite – you cannot risk anyone seeing it."

"I know," she replied softly, "oh my poor father, if he knew he was the son of Adolf Hitler, he would be devastated – and God knows what it would do to my mother – they must never know, never! Oh, Joel, I feel like something horrible knowing I have that man's blood running in my veins – I won't ever be able to risk having children, in case one of them turns out like him!"

"But, Amy," protested Joel, "You and your father are such nice people, you're nothing like Adolf Hitler."

"No, said Amy," sadly, but my brother is. Joel raised his eyebrows, "What do you mean?"

"My brother has an evil streak in him. My gran never liked him, she even cut him out of her will, because she knew. He was on the TV only the other week, opening up a home for 3rd world refugees. He hates black people, and there he was smiling and shaking hands with everyone. A week later the whole place burnt down killing most of the people. They say it was an accident, but it wouldn't surprise me if Thomas had something to do with it."

Joel stared at Amy in amazement. "Are you telling me that Thomas Kendal, the MP is your brother?"

"Yes," she replied looking at him, "didn't you know?"

"No," he replied, shaking his head in bewilderment. "Good God, Amy, they are saying that your brother is a future Prime Minister!"

"I know," she replied sickly, "Can you just imagine the grandson of Adolf Hitler being our Prime Minister? – It doesn't bear thinking about!"

She sat on the chair looking forlornly down at her muddy arms and legs. A hand went up to her hair, and she started winding strands of it round her fingers. "I look a mess," she stated sadly.

"A mess," laughed Joel, "you look like a scarecrow!" he smiled at her in mock horror. "Come here!" He took a clean handkerchief out of the pocket of his blue jeans, lifted her face with one hand and wiped the dirt and tears from her face. She looked into his eyes, which were warm and brown and smiling, and his even white teeth that showed up against his slightly tanned skin.

"Thanks, Joel," she whispered.

Amy and Joel spent the rest of the evening going through all the documents again, Joel translating everything he could. They were totally absorbed, and Amy was horrified and fascinated all at the same time. A haze of cigarette smoke hung over the table as they worked.

By midnight they were satisfied with what they had done. Joel yawned and stretched and Amy got up to make them both coffee. They both looked pale and tired.

As Amy took the coffee over to the table Joel, said, "I think I've been able to sort out what happened to your gran, although some of it will be guesswork.

"Good," said Amy.

"Are you sitting comfortably," asked Joel, trying to lighten the tense atmosphere. Amy nodded and Joel began.

"Your gran married a colonel in the Panzers, Heinrich Koner, who was either a friend or a close colleague of Adolf Hitler. Your gran and her husband had a daughter, Fransiska, and in 1940 her husband was killed. Some time later, willingly or unwillingly, she became Hitler's mistress. In 1942 she has a son by him, your father, and she calls him Heinrich after her dead husband. Whilst your father was still very young she brought him to England. We don't know whether Hitler sent her here for her own safety, or whether she came to get away from him, either way England would be the last place anyone would look for her. We know from her sister's letters that she was going back to Germany after the war. I suspect that Hitler believed that he was going to win the war, and when he was safely established as a President or a king, perhaps, he would want his son back to follow in his footsteps. I don't know what he would have done with your gran as he married Eva Braun... Maybe in his final madness he had forgotten her. I think she went to Whitechapel first, and one of her contacts got her a forged birth certificate for your father and herself. She changed her name to Caroline Kendal, as she probably felt safer keeping her same initials. She must then have got in touch with her contact in Bishops Fell, the schoolmaster, and he got her this cottage and a job at the school. We know that later she was supposed to go to America and be re-united with her family, but they must have been killed as they never got there. Your gran decided to stay here, and used the sale of the coins, probably given to her by Hitler, to get enough money to live on comfortably. What do you think, Amy?"

"I think you've got it spot on, Joel, but how does Mr Brown fit into all this?"

Joel looked thoughtful for a moment. "The only thing I can think of is that he must have worked at the antique dealers, and found out about your gran's supply of coins. When he came back from his holiday and found that she had died, he came here to try and get his hands on the rest."

"Yes, that makes sense," replied Amy, "but how much longer is he going to follow me about?"

"I can't imagine, Amy, but what ever happens we have got to get this lot locked away in the bank as soon as possible. I'll lock them in the safe in my office."

"But, Joel, said Amy wistfully, "I want to keep the photos, and I want to find out more about my gran's family. I'd like to get the death certificates of Lilli and Hans and Fransiska and gran's parents to start with."

"Amy, you cannot keep the photos, it would be too dangerous – everything has to be locked away." replied Joel firmly.

"But Joel, I could ask someone to find out without mentioning Dad, if I tell no-one about him, they won't look for him."

"OK,, Amy – but you can't risk any letters coming here from Germany, living in a village, everyone will know, it would go round like wildfire. I'll write to a researcher for you and use a P.O. Box office number for replies. I'll pay the search fee and you can pay me." Amy could have hugged him.

Thanks, Joel, you are an angel."

Joel stood up and looked at his watch. It was almost 1 o'clock in the morning.

"I'd better go now, Amy." He put his hands on Amy's shoulders. "You look all in, Amy, will you be OK?" She nodded, and a tear rolled down her cheek. Joel gently pulled her into his arms, and held her close. He kissed the top of her head, and stroked her hair.

"Oh, Joel," she cried, choked, "what ever would I do without you?" He hugged her tightly.

"Don't worry, Amy, I will be here for you always." He let her go reluctantly. He picked up his magnifying glass and dictionary and put them in the carrier bag. He turned to Amy and said, "Meet me in my office at 8.30 in the morning. We will photocopy everything in the box to save us keep handling the originals. We will lock it all up in my safe, but you will have to get another box with a key. It will be safer. When we write to the researcher we can take out the copies and replace them without touching the originals. Is that OK with you?"

"Of course," she replied.

Amy went to the door with Joel. They kissed briefly, and she stood and waved to him as he backed his car out of the drive. She locked and bolted the door and put the chain across.

Amy, although tired, put the dirty dishes into the dishwasher, and then went up to bed. She took the box up with her and tucked in under the duvet, and put her arms round it, not wanting to let it go.

It was a long time before she finally slept.

CHAPTER TEN
A LETTER TO GERMANY – AUGUST 1990

Amy slept badly that night, waking up in the morning long before her alarm was due to go off. She opened her eyes slowly, her mind blank, until she felt the metal box digging into her thigh. She closed her eyes again as the horror of the day before started creeping back into her mind. She lay for some time slowly recalling all the events, her face screwing up in anguish. She eventually lifted the duvet and looked at the box. It was still rather dirty. She had completely forgotten to clean it up and soil had marked her night-dress and the sheet. She sighed, and slowly got out of bed, leaving the box tucked under the duvet.

She drew back the curtains, put on her dressing gown, and padded slowly downstairs to the kitchen. She leaned over the sink to draw back the curtains. She was glad there was a high fence between her kitchen and Annie's cottage, it gave her a feeling of privacy. As she looked down she saw the flowers that Joel had bought her, still lying in the sink where she had left them last night. Feeling guilty she unwrapped them and put them in a vase, and placed them in the centre of the kitchen table.

She then switched on the grill, filled the kettle and made herself some toast and coffee. She sat at the table and ate her breakfast almost in a daze. Her eyes felt heavy and her head ached – she really should stop drinking brandy! She got up and took a couple of painkillers. She gazed at the clock on the wall, and suddenly remembered that she was to meet Joel in his office at 8.30. She dumped her crockery in the sink, and dashed upstairs for a quick shower and got dressed. She snatched up the box from under the duvet, wrapped it in a scarf and ran downstairs. She searched frantically for a shopping bag, and found a pretty flowered one. She pushed the box to the bottom and put her handbag on the top to hide it.

Amy set the alarm – she was close to panic as she let herself out of the cottage and into her car. She put the shopping bag on the passenger seat, and then sat and closed her eyes and prayed that Mr Brown was not hovering about waiting to follow her. She was sure that he was using the entry to the school to watch her. Eventually, pulling her self together, she switched on the car and reversed carefully into the road. She drove quickly to work, her big blue eyes constantly moving to the driving mirror to see who was behind her. Amy loved her car, which was a second hand blue mini. Now that she had got the money from her gran she would be able to go out and buy a brand new one. She would ask Joel to go with her. Dear Joel, what a tower of strength he was proving to be! Even when he had discovered that she was the granddaughter of Adolf Hitler, all he that thought about was her, trying to comfort and help her. Any other man would have run a mile.

Amy finally arrived at the bank and parked her car in the usual place behind the bank. She picked up her bag, and with trembling legs she got out and locked the door. She hurried across the sunny car park to the staff door, let herself in and went straight to Joel's office. She knocked on the door and walked in. Joel was waiting for her.

"You're on time, good girl!" he smiled. "I've got the copier warmed up, let's get moving!" Joel locked his office door, and quickly and quietly they moved over to the copier. Amy passed each document to Joel and he copied them carefully. Amy was shaking with fear in case they were disturbed. When they had finished Joel put the whole lot in the box and locked it in his safe.

"Amy,", he said earnestly, "you must get another box with a key for these originals, and we can put them in to the bank's safe with the other deposit boxes. We'll keep the copies in my safe for quick reference, as no-one else has a key, We'll need them when we write off to Germany." Joel and Amy looked at each other, and Joel wiped a hand across his brow. "Phew, thank goodness that's done!" he said, with a sigh of relief.

Joel unlocked his door. Staff were now arriving, and Amy went off to join them, after Joel had squeezed her hand and said softly, "See you later." Amy went off to the cloakroom to put away her bag. She collected her float off the chief cashier and set up her till.

Monday morning was busy as usual and Amy felt tired and wan.

"You look a bit rough this morning, Amy, are you OK?" asked Pete, who was at the next till. She grinned.

"Too many late nights," she replied.

"Oh, ho, what have you and Joel been up to?" he leered.

Amy blushed and turned back to her till to serve a customer.

All in all it was a very trying day. Joel was still trying to think who may be able to find him a researcher in Germany. He later rang a couple of friends and had to wait for a reply.

He and Amy had agreed to go to the library in Cropwell, the following Saturday morning, to see if they could find any books containing the coins they had found in he box. Amy wanted to do the search whilst her parents were still away. She was sick with worry that they would find out. She was more than thankful that they were away in Australia.

During the week Amy had been able to get a new strong box with a key. She had made sure that Mr Brown was not following her when she made the purchase. The documents were now safely stowed away in the bank's safe. Joel had recorded the deposit in his name, just in case Mr Brown had a contact in the bank.

On the following Saturday morning Amy drove to Joel's flat. He lived on the outskirts of Cropwell and was nearer to the town centre. The weather was still very hot, and Amy was dressed in a cool sleeveless, green dress and tan leather sandals. Her hair was tied back to help keep her cool.

When she arrived at Joel's flat, she parked her car outside and walked over to the intercom and pressed the button. She heard Joel say, "Come on up, Amy." The door clicked, and she went through and up the stairs. Joel's flat was on the first floor. He opened the door and let her in. Joel's flat was tidy and spacious, with the minimum of furniture and plain walls.

"Have you got a notepad and pen?" he asked.

Just a pen," she replied.

Take this, then, and put it in your bag." he said, passing her a notebook. Joel picked up his keys, and taking Amy's hand he ed her downstairs, to his car.

It didn't take long to drive into town. The weather was warming up rapidly and they had opened both windows to let in the fresh air. Joel was wearing a short-sleeved white T-shirt with his black jeans, but was still feeling hot.

When they got into the town centre Joel parked his car at the back of the main shops, and they walked the couple of streets to the library. Cropwell was an old town with large, old stone buildings. There was no modern shopping precinct, just streets of shops, offices and pubs, the police station and fire station. The hospital where Caroline Kendal had died, was a little further away on the outskirts of the town.

They arrived at the library, a tall building in dark weathered stone. They walked up the steps and through the main doors, turned and climbed the stairs to the reference library, which was surprisingly big.

The two of them wandered round the shelves looking for the coin section, when Amy suddenly gripped Joel's arm.

"What's up?" he asked puzzled. Amy's face had drained of colour.

It's Mr Brown, he's just walked in!"

"Bloody hell!" swore Joel under his breath. Amy was shaking. Joel put an arm round her waist and gently pushed her behind one of the large bookstands.

"Are you sure?" he asked quietly.

"Yes, I'm scared to death!"

"Amy, stay calm. We'll be alright as long as we keep away from the coin section. Come on, let's look for something else, and try and act natural." Joel took her trembling hand in his firm strong one, and guided her slowly round the shelves.

"Here we are, the gardening section, this will do." Amy looked vague.

"Gardening?"

"Yes," he replied, "you do want to know what to do with your garden in the autumn, don't you?" Amy nodded.

"Yes, or course," she answered slowly.

Joel selected a suitable book from the shelf, and they sat down at the nearest table. Joel made an excuse to take off his glasses and polish them so that he could look up to search for Mr Brown.

"Which one is he, Amy?" he asked softly.

"The tallish man with the mass of white hair," she whispered back. Joel looked across and saw Mr Brown, who was standing a few yards away gazing at some books.

I've seen him before," he whispered to Amy.

"Where?"

"Hanging about outside the bank," he whispered back.

"I knew he was following me!" she replied in a fierce whisper.

Amy, get the notebook out of your bag, and write down what I tell you, there's a good girl." She obeyed him silently.

Right, now here's a list of things you can plant in the autumn for the spring. First there's bulbs...daffodils...tulips, snowdrops...crocuses...and so on." Amy's hand was shaking so badly she could hardly write. Joel went on. "Winter pansies, primroses...polyanthus...heathers...lupins...they would look nice against the fence..." Joel carried on going through the book and pointing things out to Amy, whose eyes were glued to the book as she was terrified of looking up.

"OK, Amy, I think we'll make a move now. We'll leave this book on the table in case Mr Brown wants to come over and see what we have been looking at," Joel whispered.

"Where are we going?" she asked quietly.

"Another library, somewhere else," he whispered.

Joel and Amy got up from the table, and holding hands they walked leisurely out of the library. Joel looked round and said to Amy.

"We'll walk slowly along, stopping to look in the shop windows – that way we should be able to see if he's still following us. As soon as we are sure he's not, we'll go to the car and drive to Melton Mowbray and try their library."

Amy had never been so scared in her life, and said so to Joel.

"Amy, I don't think he'll hurt you. I know he has been following you about for weeks, but he has not approached you. He's just a nuisance."

As they approached Marks and Spencers Joel saw Mr Brown coming out of the library.

"Amy, quick – we'll go into Marks' and nip out at the other end. We should be able to make it to the car by the time he's got there."

They walked rapidly through Marks and Spencers. It was packed, and they had to push their way through dawdling shoppers. When they reached the far end they pushed their way through the glass doors, and ran across the road and down an alley between the shops, and within seconds they were in the car park. They got into the car and Joel eased it out towards the exit. He pushed the car parking ticket into the machine as Amy scrabbled about in her purse for some change. Joel pushed the coins into the machine and the barrier lifted. The car sped out of the car park and onto the road.

"Is he behind us?" gasped Amy.

"No," replied Joel, thankfully. He drove onto the Melton Road and put his foot down. The car sped smoothly along the winding roads. Amy and Joel opened the car windows. The car had felt like an oven when they got in. Amy dug round in her handbag and put on her sunglasses, the sun was blazing.

Joel constantly checked his driving mirror to see if they were being followed, but there was no sign of Mr Brown.

It took them about 40 minutes to get to Melton Mowbray. Joel parked the car in small car park near the market place, and they hurried to the library.

They soon found their way to the reference section and found a dozen books on coins. They went through each one carefully, but could find nothing that even resembled the Hitler coins. Amy was bitterly disappointed.

"Never mind," consoled Joel, "Let's try Smith's book shop, they might have something there."

"Good idea," replied Amy. They looked round carefully for Mr Brown, but he was nowhere in sight. They made their way to

Smith's, but all though there were a number of books on coins, there was nothing in them to help.

It was now lunch time, and Joel and Amy were hungry and thirsty. They walked round until they found a decent pub. They sat outside in the pub garden at a wooden table. Joel went into the bar and ordered them both some chicken rolls, and brought himself and Amy a glass of sweet cider. The weather was glorious, and the pub garden was full of customers who were taking advantage of the lovely weather. Amy raised her face to the sun and felt the warmth on her skin. She and Joel enjoyed their rolls and cider, and began to relax.

"What shall we do next?" asked Amy.

"I was just thinking that we could go round all the second and shops and antique shops, and see if we can find some old coin books for sale that we could have a look at." Amy agreed.

They finished their lunch and both went to toilet, which was inside the pub, and then set off.

Amy and Joel wandered round Melton Mowbray all afternoon looking in all the second hand and antiques shops. They found quite a few, but as they didn't want to draw attention to themselves by asking the shop assistants for help, they had to do all the searching themselves, going through numerous shelves and boxes, which was time consuming. Some of the books were old and dusty. There were none on coins.

By 5.30. the shops were beginning to close, and Joel and Amy were hot, dusty and tired. They were walking back to the car when Joel spotted a cafe, with a bow window looking out onto the street, and the smell of baking wafting through the open door.

"Fancy a pot of tea and a cream scone, Amy?" asked Joel.

"Oh, yes," she replied happily, "sounds wonderful."

They went into the cafe and sat in the window, and a waitress came over to take their order. When she went away, Amy took off her sunglasses and laid them on the table, and looked across at Joel.

"I'm paying for these, Joel."

"Well, I'm old-fashioned," replied Joel, "and I don't expect a woman to pay."

"Joel," argued Amy," my gran has left me a lot of money and I can afford to treat you. Anyway, I'm not just any woman, I'm your friend – we are good friends – a team."

"Okay," he replied smiling," partners." He held out his hand across the table, she took it and they shook hands. The waitress arrived with their order, giving them a funny look. Amy put a hand over her mouth to stop herself giggling. Joel looked at the waitress.

"Thank you, that was quick!" The waitress. a thin elderly woman with grey frizzy hair, merely dumped the tray on the table and walked away.

Whilst they were tucking into their cream scones and tea, Amy suddenly frowned.

"Joel, I wonder how we've managed to evade Mr Brown all afternoon?" Joel looked thoughtful.

"I wonder if he's put a 'bug' on your car?" Amy's eyes opened wide.

"Where would he get one from?" she asked horrified.

"Well, if he is a crook I should imagine he would be able to get one quite easily – it would explain things, though. He could have followed you unnoticed to my flat, but he was stuck when we went out in my car. He was able to follow us into Cropwell easily enough, but then lost us."

"Do you think he's bugged the cottage?" asked Amy nervously.

"I doubt it," he replied," because if he had he would know that the coins are locked in the bank, and are going to stay there, so it would be pointless for him to follow you around."

"Yes, that's true," she agreed slowly.

"What would you like to tomorrow, Amy?" Joel suddenly asked.

Amy had been looking at a picture on the wall of a barge on a canal.

"That," she replied, pointing to the picture. "I'd love a nice peaceful day just relaxing on one of those barges – chugging along the canal in the sunshine."

That sounds a good idea," he replied, nodding. "Isn't there a
ub somewhere that rents out barges?"

"Yes, you're right." She thought for a moment. "The Merry
oatman!" she exclaimed.

"That's the one," said Joel. "We'll have a drive over when we
ave here – we can stay for a meal and book a barge for
morrow."

The two of them finished a second cup of tea and smoked a
garette, feeling more relaxed. They eventually left the cafe and
id a peaceful drive along the country lanes.

They arrived at the 'Merry Boatman' at about 7 o'clock, just
the pub was opening. It was a beautiful, old, sprawling
iilding, with hanging baskets of flowers along the walls. There
re tables and chairs set outside right up to the canal's edge,
iere the landlord moored the barges. Amy and Joel went inside.
ie pub seemed dark after being in the bright sunshine. They
ilked up to the counter and spoke to the landlord. Joel asked if
ey could hire a barge for the next day, and how much it would
st.

You're lucky," replied the landlord," it's only so many folk
ing on holiday, that I'm not fully booked. Well, now, cost. You
n take the barge out for yourselves for £35 or you can pay £60
d have one of my boys take you out. With that you get a
rbecue and a bottle of wine plus coffee or tea during the
irney." Amy and Joel looked at each other and agreed to take
e £60 trip.

"Be 'ere for 10 o'clock," said the landlord," you gets back
out 7 o'clock, before it gets dark."

Amy and Joel looked at the menu, and decided to have
:ak, salad and chips. They paid for the meal, and trip, and
ught a drink. Amy had a glass of wine and Joel a lager.

They took their drinks outside and sat in the sunshine.
ey chose a table near to the canal edge, and watched the
rges returning. They were a hive of activity, with people
atting and unloading. The barges bumped against the canal
ge as they were tied up. The people came off the barges and
ved to tables near Amy and Joel, and began ordering food and
nks. Whilst they waited they got into conversation with Joel
d Amy, and they all sat chatting and laughing.

Eventually Joel's and Amy's meals arrived as the sun was dipping behind the trees. They sat in the warm glow of a glorious sunset.

Joel picked up Amy the following morning. He thought how lovely she looked with her shining hair stroking her shoulders, and a short blue denim dress, which showed off her slender legs. As they set off Amy mentioned to Joel the 'bug' that may be on her car.

"Do you think we should look for it?" she asked, frowning.

"Well, we would have to be careful," he replied. "We should have to be sure that Mr Brown wasn't watching us, and if we did find it, we would have to leave it, or he would know that we were on to him." Amy realised he was right.

"By the way, I have some good news," smiled Joel. "I had a phone call from one of my friends this morning. He's found us a researcher in Germany who speaks English, so we won't have to worry about translating."

"That's great," she replied, pleased.

"He does charge £10 per hour, will that be alright?" he asked.

"Of course, that will be fine." Joel went on to say that they could ask the researcher to send them some books on German coins. "Are you free tomorrow night, Amy?"

"Yes, I am," she replied.

"Well, if you want to come back to my place after work, we can get a letter sent off to Germany. I'll get the photocopies out of my safe and bring them home, then we can sort out what we have got and what we want him to find. I'll take the copies back to work the next day, and lock them away."

"That sounds wonderful!" said Amy brightening up.

Joel took a hand off the wheel, and pushed his glasses along his nose.

"Amy," he said hesitantly, "I was wondering if some time next year you would like to come on holiday with me. I thought we could tour Europe, stopping in Germany. We could search the shops for books on coins, and visit the streets where your gran and her family lived, we should have some more addresses by then. If we had a touring holiday, no-one would know that we only wanted to go to Germany." Amy's face lit up.

"Oh, Joel, that would be absolutely wonderful, I'd love to!"

She clutched his arm and leaned over to kiss him on the cheek.

Joel laughed at her enthusiasm, and thought how adorable she was.

They arrived at the "Merry Boatman" at 10 o'clock. Joel parked the car and they walked up to the pub. A young man wearing shabby jeans and a black vest met them.

"Mr Brent?" he asked. Joel nodded.

"I'm Jim, your barge is ready, I'm just stocking it up." He showed them which barge was theirs the 'Brenda' and told them to go aboard whilst he fetched the meat.

The barge was beautifully painted in red and gold, with brass fittings and tubs of flowers. The cabin had a small table and benches covered in a soft red material, and red curtains at the windows. Joel and Amy settled themselves on seats at the back of the barge and waited for Jim.

Jim soon arrived with a large cool-box. He leapt over the side of the barge and dumped the box in the cabin. He then released the mooring rope and secured it, and then switched on the engine. The barge chugged into life and slowly sailed away.

They had a lovely day. Amy and Joel sat and relaxed in the sun as the barge chugged along the water. They waved to other people in passing barges, and to people sitting along the banks, fishing. They saw ducks swim by and shoals of small fish where the water was clear. Amy made coffee for them all in the little cabin, and Jim chatted to them, showing them points of interest. It was so peaceful, it was like being in another world. At lunch time they stopped by a wooded glade, and Jim set up the barbecue, where they had steaks and kebabs on sticks with salad and fresh crusty rolls. Jim poured them glasses of sparkling white wine as they lazed in the sun.

Amy was fascinated when the barge went through the locks, seeing the water rushing in beneath the lock gates. By the time they got back to the 'Merry Boatman' Amy was relaxed and happy. It was one of the nicest days she had ever spent.

After work, the next day, Amy followed Joel back to his flat. The folder of photocopies was locked in Joel's briefcase. When they got in Joel and Amy made themselves something to eat and drink, and then went into Joel's spare room that was set up as an office for tracing his ancestors. He had a table, a couple of chairs, shelves of books, a filing cabinet and a computer, which he kept on a long table.

Joel and Amy sat at the table and he took out the copies of the documents.

"The first thing we must do is set out a chart of your family tree, from all these." He set out the papers and studied them, and then set out a tree omitting Amy's father.

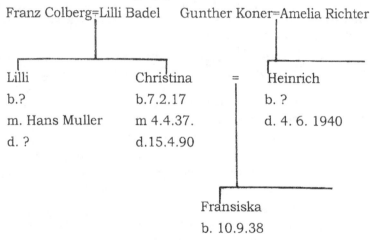

Franz Colberg=Lilli Badel   Gunther Koner=Amelia Richter

Lilli	Christina	=	Heinrich
b.?	b.7.2.17		b. ?
m. Hans Muller	m 4.4.37.		d. 4. 6. 1940
d. ?	d.15.4.90		

Fransiska
b. 10.9.38

"Right, Amy," said Joel," we've got your tree done, now we need to make a list of what we want the researcher to find. It would be best to ask him to do a few hours, then send the results and the bill. Then you pay him and ask him to do some more hours. How many hours do you want him to do at a time?" he asked.

I'll pay for ten, that will be £100," she replied.

"OK, so we'll ask him to do up to 10 hours. I'll sort out the payment through the bank, then you can owe me. Will that be alright?"

Yes, that will be fine," she replied.

They sat, heads together, and compiled a list of what they wanted found.

1. Fransiska Koner – death – 1943? Berlin

> Age about 6 years. Living with Aunt Lilli Muller.

2. Lilli Colberg –   birth – sister born 1917 – Berlin. Parents Franz Colberg and Lilli Badel. In 1917 were living Flensburgerstrasse 25. Married – Hans Muller. Before 1937.

> Death 1943?
>
> Berlin – Perlebergerstrasse 40.

3 Hans Muller   Death - as above.

4. Henirich Koner   Birth – Berlin. Died 1940 – age 30.

> Parents – Gunther Koner and Amelia Richter

5. Franz Colberg
   Lilli Badel
   Gunther Koner   want births-marriages-deaths
   Amelia Richter

"I think that's plenty to be going on with," said Amy, twisting her fingers round her hair slowly.

"Yes," agreed Joel. "We'll enclose the chart with the list."

"Joel," Amy looked at him persuadingly, "I would like to get the war records of Heinrich Koner and Hans Muller."

Joel looked round at her and ran a finger down her small nose.

"Okay, Amy, we'll put that in as well, although it may take a while to get a result."

Amy smiled at him through dark lashes as Joel weakened to her request.

Joel and Amy spent the evening writing their first letter to Germany.

CHAPTER ELEVEN
ANOTHER WAIT – AUGUST – SEPTEMBER 1990

Amy was restless. It was a Saturday afternoon, almost the end of August, and her parents were due back from Australia in two days time.

The air was hot and heavy – a prelude to a thunderstorm. Amy sat on the settee facing the window and closed her eyes. She was dreading her parents coming home. How was she going to ace her dear father, such a kind and gentle man, without giving away the terrible secret she now held? Would he be able to tell by looking at her that there was something terribly wrong?

She still could hardly believe that her father was the son of Adolf Hitler. A man who had had all those thousands of Jews and crippled children murdered during the war. She could remember Molly and Richard, her parents neighbours, going to Poland for a holiday a couple of years ago. Whilst they had been there they had gone on a visit to the concentration camp at Auschwitz. She remembered Molly telling her the horror of it, and how the birds, there, never sang. She had told her about the huge showcase full f human hair, and of another one full of suitcases with white numbers painted on them and shopping baskets scattered amongst them. There had been other showcases filled with shoes, spectacles, false limbs and baby clothes. These had all been found in the camp after the war.

Molly had gone on to tell her about the interrogation cells there people were tortured, and the standing cells, which were ny brick built cells where four people were locked in and had to stand packed together, unable to move. She had then gone on to describe the huge gas chamber were thousands of people were killed at a time. The gas chamber had been a huge brick building with vents where the gas would come through, and there was an adjoining room with two huge incinerators where the bodies were burnt.

Molly had cried all the way home.

Amy felt like crying now. It was all getting too much to bear, and the hot, heavy air was making her feel depressed, She ran her fingers through her soft hair, trying to keep it out of her face. She fanned herself with the newspaper in effort to stay cool. She really should have bought herself a fan, she scolded herself.

The phone suddenly rang. She wiped her eyes with the palms of her hands before answering it. It was Joel.

"Amy, it's Joel, are you OK?"

"I'm feeling a bit low," she replied, "I'm worried about Dad coming home and having to face him," she went on tearfully.

"Would you like me to come round now instead of later?" he asked gently.

"Yes, I would," she answered gratefully.

"I'm on my way!" he stated firmly, and put down the phone.

Joel, cancelled his game of squash, it was too hot to play comfortably anyway. He picked up his keys and went straight down to his car. He got in and opened his window – the air was hot and humid and stifling. As he drove to Amy's he saw dark, heavy clouds creeping along the sky like a great black shadow. The light was beginning to fade – a storm was on its way.

When Joel arrived at Jade Cottage he heard the first rumbles of thunder in the distance. When Amy opened the door, he took one look at her sad little face, and pulled her into his arms and held her close. She turned her face towards his and he kissed her, a long, slow loving kiss that turned her legs to jelly. She eventually looked up at him, "I needed that!" she smiled.

"So did I!" he replied warmly and hugged her again. "Poor Amy," he thought, "What a terrible burden for such young shoulders – a burden she would have for the rest of her life."

Joel and Amy moved into the living room that was growing dark. Amy put on a table lamp, and they went and sat on the window seat, by the open windows. A cool breeze had sprung up and was gently gusting through, blowing Amy's hair away from her hot face. The light outside was turning green and ominous.

The thunder grew louder and closer and great forks of lightening exploded in the sky. The rain started with great drops that smacked the ground like bullets. It got heavier and huge hailstones began to fall, covering the ground like snow. Joel and Amy hastily shut the windows and moved over to the settee facing the window. Joel took Amy's hand and they sat and watched the rain hammering down, great rivers of it pouring down the windows. They listened to its steady drumming, and watched the lightning dance wildly across the sky.

When the storm had calmed, Joel looked down at Amy, "When do your parents actually get home?" he asked.

"On Monday evening," she replied sighing.

"When will you be going round to see them?"

"Dad said he would ring me when they got in, and I said I would go straight round."

"Would you like me to come with you?" Her face lit up.

"Oh, yes please, Joel, I would. I'd feel much better if you were with me."

Joel agreed to go home with Amy after work on the Monday, so that he would be there when her father rang.

Amy snuggled up to Joel, and put her head on his shoulder. They sat in the fading light and listened to the raging storm slowly fade away.

Amy's first meeting with her father went better that she had expected. It was her mother who had phoned her to say that they were home. She told Amy that they were tired after their journey, and Amy promised that she would not stay too long. She realised that they had been travelling for over twenty-four hours, and would want to catch up on some sleep.

When Joel and Amy arrived they were met by a house full of people. Henry's friends, who had picked them up from the airport were still there, and Molly and Richard from next door, who had come round with a bag of shopping for Penny, including fresh bread and milk.

Amy and Joel were let into the house by Richard as Henry and Penny were busy chatting in the living room. When Amy walked in she was hugged by her mother.

"Amy, dear, we have missed you!" cried Penny.

"Mum, I've missed you, too. Have you had a wonderful time? So you look brown?"

"We've had a marvellous time, and the weather was gorgeous all the time. I can't understand the people who live here, they never sunbathe, and my sister is not brown at all!"

91

Penny babbled on happily. Amy looked across at her father – he looked dreadfully tired. She went across to him and hugged him.

"Hi, Dad, I've missed you, too." Henry hugged his daughter, and kissed her cheek. He was too tired to notice the anxious look in Amy's eyes.

"Hello, Amy, it's good to see you." As he spoke the telephone started ringing and Henry went off into the hall. Molly went off to the kitchen and bustled about making everyone tea and coffee.

Penny opened up a suitcase and started rummaging through for the gifts she had bought, tipping clothes out onto the floor. She fished out a beautiful, cuddly koala bear for Amy.

"Oh, Mum, he's adorable, thank you!" exclaimed Amy cuddling the soft silky toy.

"Joel, I've brought you a wallet, I thought it would be useful." smiled Penny, who had had some difficulty in knowing what to get him.

"Thank you very much, Penny. I could do with a new one," he smiled.

Penny brought out gifts for everyone, and when Molly brought in the tea and coffee, they all sat down whilst Penny happily passed round photos which she had had developed in Australia.

There were pictures of Penny's sister and husband in their big bungalow, which was set on a hill among tall palm trees, with a marvellous view of the sea, and pictures of Henry and Penny with new friends they had made, and of some of the beautiful places they had visited, such as magnificent dams, nature parks where Penny had been photographed cuddling a koala bear, stroking a tame kangaroo and one where she was covered in exotic birds! There were other lovely photos taken at Sea World, and some beautiful ones taken on a boat trip along the everglades, where the water was like a mirror.

As they were all chatting away Henry was falling asleep in his armchair, so everyone started to leave. When they had all gone Henry and Penny went off to bed, leaving their suitcases lying on the living room floor.

Amy was cuddling her koala bear in her arms as Joel drove her home.

"That wasn't too bad, was it?" asked Joel.

No," replied Amy, relieved, "the worst is over now, I shan't feel so bad the next time I see him."

When they got back to Jade Cottage Amy asked Joel if he would help her buy a new car.

What sort do you want buy?" he asked.

"Another Mini," she replied firmly.

"Another Mini?" exclaimed Joel, "don't you want something a bit grander?"

"No," she replied, "I'm hopeless at parking, but I can cope quite well with a small car." Joel laughed, his brown eyes sparkling.

"All women are hopeless at parking!"

"Also," insisted Amy, pretending to ignore his remark, "If I have got a 'bug' on my car, it's one way I can get rid of it! At least until Mr Brown finds another one."

Before Amy parted with her old Mini she and Joel gave it a good clean. It gave them the chance to look for a 'bug'. Joel eventually found one. It was a small metal disc fitted under the back bumper. It gave Amy a horrible feeling to know that her suspicions were correct. Mr Brown was most certainly on her tail!

Two weeks later Amy was the proud owner of a brand new car.

It was an other two weeks before the reply came from Germany. Joel brought the letter round to Amy's cottage after work. Amy was agog with excitement!

The researcher, a Mr Meyer, had found the birth of Lilli, her gran's sister. She had been born on 4th January, 1914, at the same address. She had married Hans Muller on 16th June, 1936, and had been killed in a bombing raid on 10th November, 1943. The address on the certificate was the same as on the letters to her grandmother - Perleberstrasse 40.

Of Fransiska, her grandmothers little girl, there was no trace. Although she had been living with Lilli, her body had not been found. Lilli's husband, Hans, must have been home on leave, as his body had also been found. He, too, had been killed on 10th November, 1943.

Mr Meyer had also found the deaths of her gran's parents. They had been killed the year before, and had lived in the same house where her gran had been born.

The certificates of all these people were enclosed. Amy was thrilled with them, but was disappointed when the researcher went on to say that most of the church records had been destroyed during the bombings, and he could not promise to get further back, but he would try. He did point out that all marriages took place at the Registry Office, and not in church.

Mr Meyer's letter went on to say that he had checked all the addresses on the certificates, but the streets were no longer the same. Most of the houses had been bombed, knocked down and rebuilt. Some of the old houses had been rebuilt as shops and offices.

He went on to say that the army records for Heinrich Koner and Hans Muller were in the Berlin Archives, and he had arranged for a fellow researcher to do the investigating on his behalf, as he had a contact in these archives, who was an expert on army research.

Amy was excited with the results. "I wonder what happened to Fransiska, my gran's little girl?" murmured Amy frowning. She felt strangely close to Fransiska, partly because she looked like her as a child, and partly because she was her father's sister. A sister he would never know about! Joel rubbed a hand across the back of his neck.

"I should imagine she must have been killed, and her body never found. She was living with her aunt, so she must have been nearby. If she hadn't been killed, she could have ended up in an orphanage, or been taken in by someone else."

"Poor little Fransiska," whispered Amy, "I wonder if she is still alive somewhere?"

Amy," said Joel quietly, "don't even think it! You cannot risk looking for her and finding her without your father learning the truth."

"I know," she replied sadly, her fingers gently twisting strands of her hair.

Joel arranged for the payment to Mr Meyer, the researcher, and asked him to continue the search for Amy's family, if it was possible.

The certificates that had arrived, Amy had reluctantly handed over to Joel to be locked safely away with all the other documents in the deed box, at the bank.

CHAPTER TWELVE

ANOTHER SHOCK FOR AMY – NOVEMBER 1990

The weeks had flown by and it was now November. The weather was cold, damp and foggy, and the days were short and dark. Amy's cottage looked warm and cosy during the winter nights, with it's flickering fire and soft lights. Amy had been thrilled at her parent's delight, when they had visited her after their holiday to Australia, and seen the decorating she had had done, and the new furnishings. Henry was very proud of his daughter's artistic talent.

One Friday night Amy had just got in from doing some shopping, when the phone rang. It was Joel.

"Amy, I need to see you, can I come round?"

"Of course," she replied. Joel sounded rather worried on the phone. "Is there something wrong?" she asked anxiously.

"Yes, I'll tell you when I see you. I'm on my way." Amy felt uneasy – what could be wrong? Had the researcher, Mr Meyer, found her father's birth certificate. Had Mr Brown done something? She felt a sense of dread. She put her shopping away, and then went to the window to watch for Joel.

The weather outside was dull and grey, the bare trees looking sad and forlorn without their lush foliage. The lights were now on in the little school opposite, and Amy felt sad. She had always hoped to have a family who would have gone to that school one day, but now she would not have children. She swallowed a lump in her throat, and her heart sank, and her blue eyes misted over in her pretty face.

Suddenly Joel's dark blue car appeared out of the light mist, and turned into her drive. She got up from the window seat and went to the door. She opened it and watched Joel get out of his car and approach her. He looked so handsome in his black polo-neck sweater and black jeans. His brown eyes looked serious, his intelligent, aquiline face troubled.

Amy, you had better sit down," he said grimly as entered the cottage. Amy was alarmed.

"What's wrong?" Joel held up a letter.

"I've just heard from Mr Meyer. The researcher in Germany, the one who agreed to find the war records of Heinrich and Hans, has been killed." Amy went cold.

"How?" she whispered, her hand going up to her hair.

"He was killed in a hit-and-run." Amy froze, her face paled.

"Do you think he was murdered?" she gasped.

"I don't know, Amy, but it is a bit of a co-incidence." Amy was horrified.

"If he's been killed, it's all my fault!" she cried.

"Amy, it may have been a genuine accident, don't start blaming yourself," he replied gently, taking her hands in his.

"This year has been a nightmare," moaned Amy - "I wish I'd never found that damned deed-box!" Joel put his arm round Amy's shoulders.

"It's not your fault, Amy." Amy started to cry.

"Joel, I can't go on like this, the burden is too much - I have to tell someone. If that man has been killed because I am tracing my ancestors, they could kill us – what are we going to do?"

"I never thought of that," Joel replied slowly, "but you could be right. I'll contact Mr Meyer and tell him to stop researching right away."

"Does he know where we live?" she asked Joel urgently.

"No, " he replied. I've been using a P.O. Box no., remember. All he knows is my name, and he knows nothing about you."

"Joel, you must be careful – I don't want anything to happen to you." Amy cried.

"I'll be OK, don't worry."

"Joel, I think we should go to the police. If that man has been murdered, we can't sit back and do nothing about it."

"The local police won't be able to do anything," replied Joel. "We'd be better off going to somewhere like Scotland Yard."

"Yes," agreed Amy. "When shall we go?"

"We can't just turn up Amy, we would have to get an appointment. We can't risk anything in writing, so I'll have to phone. Give me time to think who would be the best person to contact and I'll ring up."

"What shall we tell them?" she asked anxiously.

"I'm not sure yet, but we will have to tell them about your ancestors - I'm sure we can trust Scotland Yard to be discreet." Amy looked thoughtful.

"Joel, if we told them about Dad's birth certificate, they might be able to stop Thomas becoming Prime Minister. I don't want to hurt my brother, but the thought of him becoming Prime Minister is terrifying."

"Of course," breathed Joel, "I'd forgotten about your brother for the moment. He's getting very popular, and the newspapers are saying that it won't be long before he's at No.10."

Amy was feeling relieved that that they were going to confide in someone. She knew she would feel better if she shared her burden with someone in authority.

The letter from Mr Meyer had been a terrible shock. Amy's life had just started to settle, and there had been no sign of Mr Brown for some time, and now everything was going wrong again. Amy and Joel spent the evening going over all the facts again, but nothing had changed.

Joel was in a dilemma. He needed to find someone responsible to talk to at Scotland Yard. He did not want to risk sending a letter, and there was no-one he could ask without arousing suspicion. In the end he spent each day reading his Daily Telegraph, in the hope that he may see the name of someone suitable. He finally did. One day there was a very good article on Chief Superintendent David Clayton of Scotland Yard. Joel decide to contact him.

It took Joel some time to get hold of David Clayton on the phone, and when he did it took some time to persuade him to give them an appointment. Joel would only tell him that he wanted to discuss a very important matter, which was confidential, and that he did not want to see anyone else, or give any information over the phone. David Clayton took Joel's and Amy's names and addresses and places of work and agreed to see them the following Saturday morning at 11.30 a.m.

Joel and Amy were nervous about their meeting with David Clayton. They took with them the photocopies of the certificates,

99

the letters, the list of contacts and the newspaper cuttings, and one of the coins, as Amy was still worried that they may have been stolen or whether they were legally hers. David Clayton may be able to help.

They decided to drive down to London in Joel's car, as it would be difficult to talk to each other on the train, in front of other people. Joel checked his car before they left to make sure it wasn't bugged, and all the way to London they checked that Mr Brown was not following them.

David Clayton had had Joel and Amy checked out, and found that they were without criminal records, and were who they said they were. He was mystified as to their reason for wanting to see him.

Joel and Amy arrived at Scotland Yard and parked the car. At 11.30 they walked through the main doors, the photocopies in Joel's briefcase, and approached the counter. They spoke to a police officer on duty, and told him of their appointment. The policeman asked them their names and told them to wait. He rang David Clayton to check the appointment. He then checked Amy's handbag and Joel's briefcase – a standard security measure, and then took them up in the lift to David Clayton's office. The policeman knocked the door and a deep voice called, "Come in." The policeman opened the door for them to enter, then closed it behind them and went away.

Joel and Amy walked into David Clayton's office nervously. David Clayton went up to them and shook their hands, and asked them to sit down, pointing to two chairs facing his desk.

"What can I do for you?" he asked politely. Joel cleared his throat.

"It's difficult to know where to start, but the main reason we want to see you is to report a possible murder." David Clayton raised his dark eyebrows.

"Go on, Mr Brent."

"We recently discovered that Amy's ancestors were Nazis in Germany. We arranged for a researcher to try and find their war records in Berlin. He has been killed in a hit-and-run, but we fear that he may have been murdered." David Clayton shook his head.

"I would need more evidence than that, before I could do anything, Mr Brent," he replied. Joel looked at Amy questioningly.

"What is it you really want to tell me, Mr Brent," asked David Clayton suspiciously.

"Are you sure no-one can hear us?" asked Joel, "because we don't want anyone to hear what we are going to tell you."

"No-one can hear us, Mr Brent – now what is you problem?" Joel looked at Amy.

"I think you should tell the Chief Super., Amy." Amy looked at David Clayton, her eyes anxious. She was terrified. He knew she was afraid.

"Don't look so worried, Miss Kendal, I won't bite you," he smiled. Amy took a deep breath and briefly told him her story.

"Well," she began, her voice shaking, her hand tugging her hair, "In April this year my grandmother died and left me her cottage in Bishops Fell, which I moved into shortly after her death. In August I was digging in the garden when I found a deed box buried there. When I finally got in open I found photographs and documents in it, belonging to my gran. When I looked at them I found they were in German, so I asked Joel to come round, and with the help of a German dictionary he translated them. I...I...discovered that my grandmother and my father were born in Berlin." She stopped for a moment, and took a deep breath.

"We discovered that my grandmother had had an affair with Adolf Hitler, and that my...my...father is his son."

David Clayton could hardly believe his ears. He had not expected anything like this. He wondered if Amy was pulling his leg, but looking at the distress in her face he knew that she was sincere. He ran a hand over his hair, trying to stay calm. He broke the ominous silence.

"Do you have any proof of this, Miss Kendal?" he asked kindly. Amy nodded, and Joel took the copies and translations out of his briefcase and laid them on the desk.

Amy and Joel sat in silence as David Clayton started reading the documents. Eventually he spoke.

"Have you told anyone else about these?" he asked quietly.

"No," replied Amy, "we were too scared." Clayton continued reading, then looked across at Amy.

"So, this Heinrich Koner is your father?"

"Yes," she replied," but his name has always been Henry Kendal."

"And your grandmother?" he asked," she was Caroline Kendal?"

"Yes," replied Amy.

"So how do you know that your grandmother was this Christina Koner?"

"Because of the letters," replied Amy. "They are addressed to Caroline Kendal, but are written to Christina – and my father's date of birth is 1st March, 1942," she added hastily.

David Clayton read the translated letters, newspaper cuttings and certificates, but when he read the list of contacts, he froze. Did this couple have any idea of the enormity of their find? He was so shocked by what was lying in front of him, he was unsure what to say. Eventually he asked.

"Is this everything, Miss Kendal?"

"There were some gold coins with the head of Adolf Hitler on them," replied Joel, passing one to David Clayton as Amy continued.

"We have been trying to find about them, but we've not had any luck."

"Where are the originals of these documents, and the rest of the coins?" he asked them.

"They are locked away at the bank where we work," Amy answered.

"I suggest you keep them there," suggested David Clayton carefully. "Now, Miss Kendal, I take it that your father knows nothing about all this?"

"Oh, no," gasped Amy, shocked. "I could never tell him, ever."

"Do you have any brothers or sisters, Miss Kendal?" asked David Clayton curiously.

"Yes, she replied uneasily, "I have a brother."

"And what does he do?" Amy took a deep breath.

"He's a member of parliament," she replied, her inside turning over, her hands trembling.

The silence was deafening. For a moment David Clayton was speechless. He looked at Amy and frowned.

"Are you telling me that Thomas Kendal, the MP is your brother, and the grandson of Adolf Hitler?"

"Yes, I am," she replied, her lips trembling.

David Clayton's mind was racing. Never in his career had he faced a situation like this. He looked at Amy's white face and her trembling hands.

I expect you are concerned about your brother becoming Prime Minister one day?" he said to Amy gently.

"Yes," she stammered, "I am."

"Well, I shouldn't worry if I were you. Your brother is a popular and capable MP and his generosity to people is well-known. Some people have already nick-named him Saint Thomas.

"But that's just the point," cried Amy, "he's not like that at all, it's all a facade!" she stopped, feeling uncomfortable.

"What do you mean exactly, Miss Kendal?" asked David Clayton, puzzled.

"Well, for a start, he's given money to homes for third-world refugees, crippled children and down-and-outs, but he hates them! Even when we were children he was the same. He hates everyone who is not white and perfect. When we were young he would cross the road rather than walk past a disabled person or someone in a wheelchair, and I can remember a horrible story about him when he was at school."

"What was that?" interrupted David Clayton in a voice that wasn't quite steady.

"When I was school I had a friend whose brother was in Thomas's class. In their class they had a coloured boy called Sukraj. He was an intelligent and polite boy, who came from a good family - his father was a doctor. Anyway, Thomas hated him because he was black. Suddenly Thomas made friends with him, and they became good pals. Well, one day something terrible happened, and Sukraj got into terrible trouble and was expelled, I think it was something to do with drugs. Everyone was sorry for Thomas, because they were friends, but my friend's brother insisted that Thomas had set him up to get rid of him." Amy stopped, feeling guilty.

By now David Clayton's heart was racing. It took all his self-control not to let Joel and Amy see how worried he was.

"If that's the case, Miss Kendal, we'll just have to make sure that your brother does not get to No.10, so please don't worry."

Joel spoke up at this point.

"Are you going to do anything about the man killed in Germany?" he asked politely.

"What was his name, Mr Brent?" Joel looked uncomfortable.

"We don't know, Sir."

"Perhaps you could explain, Mr Brent?"

Joel did explain to him that he had written to a researcher, a Mr Meyer, to trace Amy's ancestors, and to find the war records of Heinrich Koner and Hans Muller. Mr Meyer wrote to say that he had asked a colleague to do the army research as he had a contact in the Berlin Archives. It was the second researcher who had been killed.

"I see," replied David Clayton nodding his head slowly, his big fingers gently tapping his desk. "Do you think the second researcher had yours or Miss Kendal's addresses?"

"No," replied Joel, "I have kept Amy out of it. I have used a P.O. Box number for replies, and Mr Meyer only had my name."

David Clayton nodded again, and wrote something down on a piece of paper, and handed it to Joel.

"Mr Brent, please take these telephone numbers – one is the direct line to this office, and the other is my home number. If you or Miss Kendal feel that you are in any danger, contact me at once."

"Thank you," replied Joel, relieved.

At that moment a telephone on the desk rang, and David Clayton picked up the receiver and spoke into it,"...speaking ...I'm still rather busy at the moment...please ask him to wait a few more minutes...thank you..." He looked at Joel and Amy.

"I'm sorry about that, but I have another appointment." Amy and Joel started to rise.

"Please," said David Clayton, "don't get up just yet. I want you to know that I am going to refer your case to Special Branch. I will have to give them these documents and the coin, which they will return to you. Is this alright with you, Miss Kendal?"

"Yes, or course," she replied.

"They will be quite safe, I assure you," he continued. I will contact Andrew Shaw, the Head of Special Branch and he will be in touch with you. I shall also have to ask you to sign the Official Secrets Act – I shall arrange this with Mr Shaw. And, Miss Kendall, I must warn you, and you, Mr Brent, to keep totally silent about all you have found. If the press ever got hold of your story they would hound you and your family for the rest of your lives."

"Yes, we understand," nodded Amy.

As they stood up to go David Clayton warned Amy to do no more research.

"Miss Kendal, let sleeping dogs lie."

He shook their hands, and thanked them for coming to see him. He opened the door, and showed them where to find the lifts.

As they went down in the lift Amy suddenly exclaimed.

"We didn't tell him about Mr Brown or the burglary!"

"We didn't have any more time, Amy, but we can tell this Andrew Shaw when he contacts us," replied Joel.

"Oh, yes, of course," sighed Amy. relieved.

When they finally got outside, Amy breathed another sigh of relief.

"I feel much better for having got that lot off my chest."

"So do I," rejoined Joel. "Come on, Amy, let's go and find a nice pub and have a meal and a drink."

"Good idea!" she replied, and holding hands they walked away from Scotland Yard.

Meanwhile, in his office David Clayton was sitting at his desk, still reeling from the shock of Amy's visit, and what he had discovered. He picked up the receiver of one of his many phones and rang Andrew Shaw.

"Andrew, David here. I need to see you as soon as possible, in private. Can you come to my home tonight at 8 o'clock?"

"That bad, huh?" replied Andrew Shaw.

"Yes," answered David Clayton tersely.

"I'll be there," came the firm reply.

David Clayton had one more appointment before lunch, who was already waiting. After he had seen him David Clayton decided to check on Thomas Kendal's background. He had to make sure that Amy was telling the truth, before he could make any further decisions.

David Clayton gathered up the copies of the documents and the coin, and put them back into Joel's folder, and locked them in one of the drawers in his desk. He sat and gazed at the door in which Amy had not long gone through. "Poor little Amy," he thought to himself. "What a terrible discovery she has made, and what a shame she has just, possibly, signed her brothers' death warrant!

Andrew Shaw arrived at David Clayton's house at exactly 8 p.m. The two men had been good friends for many years, being in the army together in their younger days and joining the police force at the same time.

David's wife, Margaret, had gone to the theatre with friends, and his two sons were at university, so the house was conveniently empty. David Clayton ushered his friend into the house and took him to his 'den'.

"What's up, David?" asked Andrew.

"Sit down, Andrew, and have a drink, you are going to need it." David poured them both a whisky and the two men sat down in the two armchairs, either side of the gas fire, which threw out a cosy warmth.

"Well?" asked Andrew.

"I've got a prime suspect for our run of 'accidents'."

"Who?"

"Thomas Kendal," stated David gravely.

"The MP? You've got to be kidding!" scoffed Andrew.

"I'm afraid not, Andrew. His sister came to see me this morning. She has evidence that she and Thomas are the grandchildren of Adolf Hitler!

"What!" shouted Andrew, nearly spilling his drink. "I don't believe it!"

David went on to tell Andrew all about his interview with Amy and Joel. He showed him the documents and the gold coin. Andrew Shaw was horrified.

"Are you sure this girl is on the level? She could be a nut-case!" demanded Andrew.

"I've had her checked out. She is Thomas Kendal's sister and I believe her."

"But just because Thomas is the grandson of Hitler, it doesn't mean he's a murderer!" David went on to tell Andrew about Amy's story and her true opinion of Thomas. He looked hard at Andrew.

"What the hell are we going to do?" questioned Andrew Shaw rubbing a hand across his chin.

"First of all we'll have to tell the Home Secretary and convince him, then get an interview with the P.M. as he wants to know everything that's going on. Then we'll have to put a 24 hour watch on Thomas Kendal, and see who he contacts, and get a tap out on his phone." Andrew nodded in agreement David Clayton continued.

"Andrew, I'd like you to go and see Amy and get the full story from her and her boyfriend. Can you also see if you can find out anything about this gold coin, she has another seven of them. We need to know whether they were stolen or whether they are legally hers. I'll try and find out about this possible murder in Berlin." Andrew Shaw nodded.

"Of course."

"I've told them they will have to sign the Official Secrets Act."

"I'll get that done when I go see them," replied Andrew. "I'll make sure they keep quiet."

"Thanks, Andrew." Andrew Shaw looked thoughtful, and looked across at David Clayton.

"You know, David, that girl may need some protection. I've got a contact in Cropwell, and old army friend of my father's. He's retired now, of course, a good chap. I'll get him to keep an eye on Amy Kendal – his name is Charles Brown.

CHAPTER THIRTEEN
ANOTHER MEETING AT NO. 10

The two men talked late into the night, drinking whisky and smoking cigars. Their biggest worry was going to be to persuade the Prime Minister and the Home Secretary that Thomas Kendal might be their prime suspect for the accidental 'murders'.

"We have enough evidence to prove that he is the grandson of Adolf Hitler," said David Clayton, "but nothing to prove that he is organising these murders – all we have is his sister's word that Thomas is acting out a charade, and all his good works are a pretence."

"What do you think he is up to, David?" asked Andrew Shaw.

"It's pretty obvious to me," growled David Clayton, "he's another Hitler and wants to get rid of all the minority groups. He's trying to stir up the public to his way of thinking, and when they do – bingo! He will step in as their saviour and do it, and everyone will love him."

"It could take a long time to do that," replied Andrew Shaw, rubbing his chin with a beefy hand.

"Yes, but he's got time, he's only about 30 years old now," mused David Clayton.

"You could be right, David. Imagine the power he would have as Prime Minister. No wonder his sister is so worried."

"Mmm...she knows what he is really like," agreed David Clayton. "Andrew," he urged, "get as much as you can out of that girl. We cannot risk asking anyone else about Thomas's character, the fewer people who know about our suspicions the better."

During the evening Margaret Clayton returned home from the theatre. She came into the 'den' turning her nose up at the cloud of smoke that hit her as soon as she walked in.

"Hello, you two, would like some supper?" she smiled.

"Yes, please, dear," replied her husband, rubbing his hands together.

"Enjoy your show, Margaret?" asked Andrew.

"Yes, thanks, it was lovely."

"What did you see?"

"Starlight Express."

"Is that the one where everyone's dressed like a train and whizzes round on roller skates?"

"Yes, that's the one!" laughed Margaret.

"God forbid! What will they think of next!" smiled Andrew Shaw shaking his head.

Margaret Clayton went off to the kitchen to get the two men some ham sandwiches and coffee. She was an attractive woman, tall and fair and rather thin, unlike Andrew's wife who was small dark and motherly.

A few minutes later she returned with their supper and placed it on the coffee table that David had drawn up to his chair.

"I'm going to bed now, David, nice to have seen you, Andrew."

The men wished her goodnight, and she sailed out of the room. They sat in silence and ate their supper, and when the house was again still and quiet, they continued their talk.

Andrew frowned and leaned forward stabbing his finger into the air." David, do you remember that home where all the disabled children were gassed?"

"I do indeed," replied David Clayton, shuddering at the memory of it.

"Well," continued Andrew Shaw, "I'm sure that Thomas Kendal was at the opening of it. He'd donated a few thousand pounds towards the renovations."

"Yes, that's right," agreed David Clayton" he did the same for one of the homes for third world refugees and the down-and-outs which all got burned down, and I'm sure there's been more."

Andrew Shaw looked puzzled, "Do you think he would donate money to a place and then have it destroyed? He must be mad!"

"So was Adolf Hitler," replied David quietly.

They sat in silence for a few moments, thinking, until David Clayton spoke again. "We're not getting anywhere with the murders of these child abusers, are we?"

"No," replied Andrew," but it's almost impossible to do proper enquiries without arousing people's suspicions. The P.M. is making our job very difficult."

"If someone is going round murdering these people, he must be getting paid, Thomas Kendal and his wife are loaded. He could easily pay. No-one is going to go around killing people for nothing."

"Well," pondered Andrew Shaw," We've checked all the families of the children who were abused or killed. All the decent families seem to be no better off financially, and the not so decent families don't seem to be flashing any money about. We've had them all followed in turn, and not one of them has done anything out of the ordinary, or been in the vicinity of another murder. He must be paying an outsider."

"We could go on for ever in circles without a breakthrough, perhaps we should concentrate on the mass murders," suggested David Clayton.

"I suggest," said Andrew Shaw," that on Monday we go through all the newspapers for the last couple of years. We've got a list of all the destroyed buildings. We can find all the ones that Thomas Kendal attended and mark them off. Then we can re-check all the companies who did the refurbishments, and see if we can tie anything up or if Thomas Kendal had any connection with them."

"Good idea," rejoined David," and I'll contact George Daker to get us an appointment with the P.M. – he'll have to be told as soon as possible. I'll cancel all my appointments for Monday."

"Right," agreed Andrew Shaw, "I'll do the same. Can you be at my office at about 9 o'clock?"

"Yes," replied David, "I'll try and get that appointment sorted with the P.M. before I come."

David Clayton picked up the 'list' of contacts that Amy had found. "What are we going to about this, Andrew?"

111

Andrew Shaw took the list off David Clayton and studied the list of names that had been given to Caroline Kendal when she had come to England. He pursed his full lips and rubbed a hand over his chin which was beginning to feel rough with it's ginger stubble. "These people are either German spies or English traitors. They could all be dead by now. I can hardly believe that there are three people from the Cropwell area on this list – a little country town. How did they get away with it? I shall have to get all these people checked out to see who is still alive, and who has died. It would be difficult to arrest these people without dragging young Amy and her family into it. I don't want any harm to come to that lassie."

David agreed. "Perhaps it would be best to decide when we know who is alive, and who isn't." Andrew nodded.

"Yes, you're probably right. He yawned and stretched, and looked at his watch – it was gone midnight. He is eased his bulk out of the armchair. "Christ, I think I'd better get a taxi home, after all that whisky – I'll collect my car in the morning."

David Clayton slowly stood up. "No problem," he replied.

The two men walked into the hall, and David Clayton rang for a taxi for his friend. "You working tomorrow, Andrew?"

"No," replied Andrew Shaw, "We are going to my little granddaughter's birthday party. She's two tomorrow."

"Ah, the little one with the red hair and green eyes!" laughed David Clayton.

"That's the one. She looks like me, the poor little bugger!"

Andrew Shaw adored his granddaughter. She was the only grandchild who had inherited his colouring.

"I'll see you in the morning, when you pick up your car, Andrew. I'll lock up those documents and bring them along on Monday morning."

"Right you are" replied Andrew, as he left the house, his taxi having arrived. The two men said goodnight.

David Clayton went back in to his den. He switched off the gas fire and locked the documents in his briefcase, and wearily climbed the stairs to bed.

The two men slept badly that night. Amy Kendal's burden was now on their shoulders.

Many miles away in Bishops Fell, Amy was nestled snugly in her bed, fast asleep. She and Joel had spent an enjoyable day together in London.

After leaving Scotland Yard they had found a decent pub, and enjoyed a ploughman's lunch and a drink, and decided to do a little sightseeing whilst they were in London. Eventually they decided to go and visit the Tower Of London, as neither of them had ever been. They hailed a taxi and set off for London's famous fortress.

They stood in a long queue, and shivered in the cold sun. Joel was wrapped in a warm overcoat over his suit, and Amy looked attractive in a long navy cord skirt and white fluffy high necked sweater. She was wearing an expensive navy three-quarter jacket, which she pulled round her to keep warm.

They eventually got through the turnstile and into the grounds. Amy was amazed at the scene before her.

"Gracious!" she exclaimed, "I thought the tower was just a tower, I didn't realise it was inside a great castle!" Joel smiled and took her arm. They wandered happily round the buildings and through the grounds. They went up the famous tower where many famous and infamous prisoners had spent their last days, and down to the jewel house, where the crown jewels were kept in glass showcases, and guarded by Beefeaters. Amy loved the fabulous royal crowns and orbs and jewellery, but was gently pushed along the walkways by the crowds. They finished their trip with a visit to the souvenir shop – 'A magnet for women' was Joel's remark. Amy bought a bookmark, some stationery and some sweets, and then the two of them set off to find a taxi to take them back to Scotland Yard.

When they left the Tower of London it was dark and very cold. A taxi took them to the car park near Scotland Yard, and they set off home. It was a long drive through the crowded London streets. Amy gazed at the tall buildings and brightly lit shops, and the hoards of people who pushed and shoved their way along the crowded pavements. Where on earth did all these people come from?

They finally got out of London and on to the M1. Joel drove quickly along the busy motorway, and when they halfway home he pulled into a service station, where they both tucked into a hot meal and a drink.

When they left the restaurant Amy bought a bunch of flowers to put on her gran's grave, and they stepped outside to a cold, clear night. Bright stars were twinkling in a black velvety sky, and the frost on the cars was sparkling in the moonlight. Joel cleared the car windows and put on the heater to warm the car, and put in a cassette of soft music. Amy was asleep long before she got home. When they got back to Jade Cottage, Joel stayed for a coffee, then kissed Amy goodnight, and set off home. Amy climbed the winding staircase up to her bedroom, wondering what David Clayton was going to do after her visit.

She had no idea that her brother was already following in his grandfather's footsteps.

On the Monday morning David Clayton arrived at Scotland Yard early. He rang George Daker, the Home Secretary, but he had not arrived. He spoke to George Daker's secretary.

"Could you ask him to ring me as soon as he comes in, please. I shall be in Andrew Shaw's office in Special Branch. It is urgent."

"Certainly, Sir," she replied.

David rang Andrew to tell him he was on his way. When he got there some of Andrew's staff were already bringing up piles of newspapers.

"Morning, Andrew."

"Ah, there you are, David. I've got the last year's papers coming up now. The previous year is on microfilm, I've got that and a reader on its way up."

"Good God!" exclaimed David, "It will take us for ever to get through this lot!"

"I know, and I've got Peter Malcolm up in Wolverhampton investigating another 'accident'. A huge juggernaut has crashed into a mosque, killing dozens of praying Indians. The driver is in hospital, suffering from internal injuries and shock. As soon as Peter rings me I'll tell him to get straight back here, so if you can help me just for today I'd be grateful."

"Of course," replied David, taking off his jacket and settling himself at the table.

The two men could have done with some assistance, but did not want anyone else to know of their suspicions of Thomas

114

Kendal. When all the newspapers and the film and reader had arrived Andrew Shaw told his secretary not to disturb them, unless there was an emergency. The two men settled down and started going through the papers, making notes.

The hours crawled by, but nothing came to light. Some of the 'accidents' had no connection with Thomas Kendal at all. He had attended about half of them. The contractors were all from different companies, and there was no pattern whatsoever. They checked on the people connected with the companies, such as directors and shareholders, but there was no sign of Thomas Kendal.

"There's nothing here," sighed Andrew Shaw. "How on earth could he have fixed these accidents?"

"Perhaps we're wrong, and he's totally innocent," suggested David Clayton, but he felt in his heart that was not so.

"During the morning George Daker had phoned David Clayton.

"What's the problem, David?" he had asked.

"We've got a prime suspect, Sir."

"Who is it?"

"I'd rather not say on the phone, Sir, but we do need to see the P.M."

"Right, I'll arrange an appointment for us, and you can fill me in on the details."

The Home Secretary had contacted the Prime Minister, and they were to see him at 9.30 p.m. that evening. Peter Malcolm had also rung in and agreed to be in the following morning.

By 7 p.m. David Clayton and Andrew Shaw were exhausted.

"God, I'm knackered," yawned Andrew. "Let's go off to the 'Victory' and get some grub and a pint."

"Me, too," sighed David scratching his head. He closed his eyes and stretched.

"We can have a walk down and get a breath of air, and I'll get my driver to pick us up and take us to no.10."

Andrew Shaw contacted his driver, and the two men freshened themselves up, and shared Andrew's electric shaver.

They then walked to the 'Victory'. The pub was warm, busy and full of smoke. The two men found a table in the corner of the lounge and ordered a hot meal. Steak and kidney pie and chips and a couple of pints of beer made them both feel human again!

At 9.30 p.m. the two men were once again being shown into No.10. The night was cold and misty and they were glad to be let into the warmth of No.10 by a member of staff who took them up to Howard Markham's office. George Daker had already arrived.

"Good evening, Gentleman," smiled Howard Markham pleasantly. "I understand you have made some progress with our 'problem'"

"Yes, Sir," replied David Clayton, "we now have a prime suspect."

"Well, who is it?" demanded the Prime Minister. David and Andrew exchanged glances.

"Thomas Kendal, Sir," stated David, tapping his slender fingers on the briefcase that was lying on his lap.

"What!" gasped the Prime Minister. "You don't mean Thomas Kendal, one of my best politicians?"

"Yes, Sir, I'm afraid we do," replied David, his face grim.

"This is ridiculous, outrageous!" he stormed.

The Home Secretary looked thunderstruck. "What possible reason could you have for thinking such a thing?" he glared.

Andrew spoke up.

"Would the fact that we have discovered that he is the grandson of Adolf Hitler, be a good enough reason, Sir."

"Don't talk rubbish!" snapped George Daker. Howard Markham turned pale.

"Perhaps you would like to explain, Gentleman," Howard Markham stated coldly.

David Clayton and Andrew Shaw told them all they knew and all they suspected. The Prime Minister sat rigidly in his chair, stroking his silk tie whilst David Clayton was telling him about Amy's visit. He frowned and nodded his head as they finished.

"This is dreadful," his voice shook, "dreadful" He continued stroking his tie, then looked up and across at David Clayton.

"Do you have these documents?"

"Yes, Sir," replied David, taking them out of his briefcase and passing them over to Howard Markham. The P.M. put on his glasses and read through the documents carefully. He finally looked up, his face sad, his voice strained.

"There is no doubt about his parentage, and I can understand why he is your prime suspect, although I think you are probably wrong I realise we cannot dismiss the possibility, though, what measures do you want to take?"

Andrew Shaw leaned his big body forward. "We would like a 24 hour watch on him, Sir and a tap on his phone."

"Fair enough," replied Howard Markham, "but I don't want anyone to know that Thomas Kendal is the grandson of Adolf Hitler."

"We wouldn't let that happen, Sir," replied Andrew Shaw. "We'll tell my men that we have had a tip off that Thomas Kendal's life may be in danger, and they are to watch and photograph everyone he meets. We can tell them Thomas does not know about the threat, and is not to know they are watching."

"Very well, "agreed the Prime Minister, "but I don't know how you are going to tap his phone from inside the house. I have been to Thomas's house a number of times, and there is always someone in. Firstly there is his wife, then there is a live-in housekeeper and her husband. They live in rooms on the top floor. The housekeeper does all the cooking and cleaning, and her husband is Thomas's chauffeur, butler and general dogsbody. They are both devoted to Thomas. The shopping is sent out for and delivered, so the housekeeper hardly ever leaves the house. During most of the year Thomas had a gardener, who potters round the garden and goes into the kitchen for meals. The house is just never empty."

"That's no problem, Sir," replied Andrew Shaw, trying to keep a straight face, "we can tap into it from outside."

"Of course, silly of me," blustered the Prime Minister, looking uncomfortable. "Gentlemen, I want a regular report on this. You can contact me directly if necessary. I want utmost discretion in this matter."

"What do we do if we find him guilty, Sir" asked Andrew, his green eyes watchful.

The P.M. looked steadily at Andrew Shaw.

"That's your department, Andrew," was his reply. "I want no scandal – None!"

The following morning Peter Malcolm was back in London, and arrived at the office to find his boss snowed under with newspapers.

"What's going on?" he asked puzzled.

"You'd better sit down, Peter, and I'll explain." The two men had a lengthy conference. Peter Malcolm was dumbstruck when he heard the news.

"Bloody hell, Andrew, it's unbelievable!" he breathed, running a finger over his neat little moustache.

"I know," replied Andrew, "but it's a fact. Now we have got to go through the rest of these newspapers, and don't forget, no-one else is to be told under any circumstances."

"When are we starting surveillance?" asked Peter.

"I'm holding a meeting at 4 o'clock, and we can start discussions. Now how did it go in Wolverhampton?"

"I didn't get much. The driver was a white man, middle-aged. All he said was that he couldn't remember a thing. Thinks he must have had a blackout."

"What are his injuries?"

"Cuts and bruises, and a cracked rib."

"What about his circumstances?"

"He's a widower. His wife died of cancer a few years ago. He lives on his own. Seems an ordinary sort of guy."

"It's always the same," frowned Andrew Shaw, shaking his head.

That afternoon Special Branch began to organise their plans for watching Thomas Kendal. The Prime Minster was so upset, he kicked the Downing Street cat!

CHAPTER FOURTEEN
A VISIT FROM SPECIAL BRANCH – DECEMBER 1990

Amy was relieved to have been to Scotland Yard. She felt a great weight had been lifted from her shoulders. Unfortunately her fear returned when she realised that Mr Brown was back!

She confided her fears to Joel, but he said, "Don't worry, Amy, we'll tell Special Branch when they come to visit you." Amy was still feeling uneasy, and waited anxiously for them to contact her. By the end of that week Amy got a phone call from David Clayton. He phoned one evening after she had got home from work.

"Miss Kendal, this is David Clayton speaking."

"Oh, hello, Chief Superintendent."

"How are you?"

"I...I'm fine thank you."

"Miss Kendal, I have passed your case on to Special Branch, as I mentioned on your visit, and Andrew Shaw, the Head of Special Branch, and a colleague, would like to come and see you. Would next Tuesday at 7.30 be convenient?"

"Yes, yes, that would be fine."

"Could you also ask Mr Brent to come to this meeting?"

"Yes, of course."

"Have you heard anything at all from Germany?"

"No, nothing."

"That's good. Please take care, Miss Kendall, and don't hesitate to call me if you have any problems."

"Thank you very much."

"Goodbye, Miss Kendal."

"Goodbye, and thank you."

Amy rang Joel and told him about the meeting the following Tuesday, and he agreed to be there.

"Joel," said Amy slowly, "What shall I do if my mum and dad turn up whilst Special Branch are here?" Joel thought for a moment.

"Do they often turn up out of the blue?"

"Well, no, they usually phone first."

"Then don't worry, if they phone you just say you are going out, otherwise we'll just have to keep our fingers crossed that they don't turn up."

Amy was still worried and nervous, and by the Tuesday was a bag of nerves. She was glad to get away from the bank in case anyone noticed how distracted she was feeling. She had received another large cheque from the solicitor the day before, and she had had to go to the Building Society during her lunch hour to deposit it. She was still amazed at her new-found wealth, and the fact that there was still more to come.

Amy hated the winter. It was cold and dark when she left work, and she had to put the heater on in her car to warm it up and clear the windows. She drove through Cropwell slowly. The roads were busy at this time of day. By the time she left Cropwell and was driving along the country lanes to Bishops Fell, a mist had come down and she could hardly see. She drove along very slowly, her eyes straining. The mist was in patches, floating like ghosts from field to field. She was thankful when she finally saw the street lights of Bishops Fell, glowing like fuzzy beacons in the sky.

She parked her car and went into the cottage. The central heating was on and the cottage felt warm and welcoming. She put on lights, the TV. and the gas fire, and drew the curtains. The flickering flames of the fire made the room come to life, and gave it a cosy feeling. Amy heated up a pizza in her microwave and made herself a hot drink, then with trembling fingers she fished out a packet of cigarettes from her handbag, and lit up. She drew in the smoke thankfully, and felt a little calmer.

By 7 o'clock Joel had arrived, and they sat in the living room waiting for Andrew Shaw and his colleague. Amy poured them both a glass of wine, and they both lit a cigarette.

"Are you OK?" frowned Joel, looking at Amy.

"Yes...I wonder what he will say, and what he will be like, this Andrew Shaw?"

"No idea. Who is he bringing with him?"

"I don't know, David Clayton just said a colleague."

"We must remember to tell him about your burglary, and about Mr Brown," urged Joel.

"I know, I mustn't forget this time." she replied. They sat in silence.

"They're late," murmured Amy beginning to fret "It's gone 7.35."

"Don't worry, Amy" soothed Joel. "They are probably delayed by the weather, it's awful out there tonight."

At 7.45. p.m. they heard a knock at the door. With her heart hammering, Amy went to answer it. She opened the door to see two men standing there. The first, a tall thick-set man with a ginger crew cut, spoke to her.

"Miss Kendal?"

"Yes," she stammered.

"Good evening. My name is Andrew Shaw, you are expecting me."

"Yes, of course, please come in." She stood aside and let in the two men. The second man took off his hat to reveal a thatch of thick white hair.

"Mr Brown!" gasped Amy, her eyes flew open, and a hand went to her throat. "What are you doing here?"

"Andrew Shaw spoke to her, pointing at the living room door.

"Do we go in here?"

"Yes...yes.." stammered Amy, reeling from the shock of seeing her enemy. They all walked into the living room. When Joel saw Amy's white face, and then saw Mr Brown behind her, he stood up.

"What's going on!" he demanded angrily.

"It's alright, Mr Brent," replied Andrew Shaw. "Believe me, Charles Brown is a friend – not an enemy."

Joel and Amy were horrified at the sight of Mr Brown. They sat down together on the settee facing the window, Joel taking

121

Amy's shaking hand in his firm one. Andrew Shaw and Charles Brown sat on the settee facing the glowing fire.

Joel was angry. He glared at Andrew Shaw.

"We want and explanation!" he demanded.

Andrew Shaw looked across at Charles Brown. "Charles, I think you had better explain before we go any further."

Charles Brown looked across at Amy, his blue eyes twinkling.

"I'm sorry if I have frightened you, Amy, but please believe me when I say that I have been trying to protect you."

Amy looked at him in amazement, her blue eyes wide, a hand twisting her hair.

I really was a friend of your grandmother's, Amy. I first met her in Germany, before the war. I was a young soldier stationed over there. I met Christina on a number of occasions, and her sister, Lilli. We weren't close then, but we were on speaking terms."

Amy's eyes began to light up, her curiosity rising.

"Well, many years later I was in Cropwell, when I bumped into her, and she recognised me. We stopped to talk to each other, and she begged me not tell anyone that she was from Germany. She had changed her name to Caroline Kendal. She had her little son, Henry, with her in England, and even he didn't know that he had been born over there. Caroline and I often bumped into each other over the years, and she was always grateful that I had kept her secret safe, and she trusted me."

Amy and Joel sat in silence, their eyes glued to Charles Brown, hardly able to believe what they were hearing. Charles leaned forward and continued.

"A few years ago she confided in me and asked me to do something for her. She told me that in her cottage she had some documents and photos of her past life. They included a photo of her precious daughter, Fransiska, her sister Lilli and her husband, and her parents. She had already arranged for you to have her cottage after her death, and she didn't want you to find them. I told her to destroy them, but she refused, saying she couldn't bear to part with them. We finally agreed, that if she died before me, I would come to this cottage, as soon as I heard of her death, get the documents from their hiding place, and destroy them. She also gave me a key. Well, as you know, your grandmother died whilst I was on holiday."

Tears shimmered in Amy's eyes as she thought of her grandmother's distress. She clutched Joel's hand tightly.

"I came to the cottage to find the documents, but found that you had already moved in. You can imagine how shocked I was. I was terrified that you would find the documents before I did. I did not know exactly what they all were, but I did know that your grandmother and Lilli had married Nazis, and that they were all close friends of Hitler, and your grandmother was quite adamant that you were never to see them." Charles Brown ran a hand through his thick white hair, and shifted in his seat.

"I watched the cottage for a few days, as I needed to know what times you went out and came back. One day you threw out a black bag of rubbish. I looked in it and saw that it was full of old papers. I took it and searched through it, in case you had thrown them away without realising what they were. Of course, they weren't there. The next day I let myself into the cottage and went to the hiding place which was under the floorboards in the corner of her bedroom. You can imagine my horror when I found they had gone. I was frantic. I searched the cottage from top to bottom, but I still couldn't find them. I'm not a very good burglar, I'm afraid, and that evening you called the police. I was still not sure if your grandmother had already destroyed them or whether you had found them, so I have been following you about, in case you had found them and started asking questions. I must say, my, you were very careful."

Amy was dumbfounded, but relieved.

"That explains a lot!" she exclaimed, "but why are you here with Mr Shaw?" Andrew Shaw spoke up then.

"We were a little worried about your safety, Amy, may I call you Amy? I have known Charles Brown all my life. He was in the army with my father, and I know you can trust him completely. I asked him to keep an eye on you, after your meeting with David Clayton. When we met earlier this evening he put me in the picture!"

"Well, what an amazing coincidence," cried Amy. "Does Mr Brown know everything?" she asked Andrew Shaw. He nodded.

"He does now, Amy. I wanted someone near you who could be trusted, and he had to know the facts."

Amy looked across at Charles Brown. "You say you knew my gran's sister – what was she like?" Charles Brown smiled.

"She was a lovely girl, Amy, fair-haired and blue eyed and so pretty, just like your grandmother. She was so full of life and friendly. She and your gran were very close and went everywhere together. Even their husbands were best friends."

"What else can you tell me about them?" she asked eagerly.

"I don't think we have enough time for that now, Amy. I'll visit you again, and we can have a chat."

Andrew Shaw broke in at this point and said kindly to Amy.

"Amy, I would like you tell me all the events that have happened since your grandmother died. Please take your time, so that I can digest all the information."

Amy took a deep breath and began to tell him her story. Andrew Shaw listened carefully, occasionally nodding his head, the tape recorder hidden in his pocket slowly turning.

When Amy had finished Andrew Shaw asked her many questions about Thomas. Amy explained to him that her brother was quite a lot older than herself, and she had not had much to do with him since he had left home and gone to London. He had always treated her kindly as a child, playing with her, giving her 'piggy backs' and reading her stories. It was only as she got older that she realised that Thomas only liked people who, in his eyes, were perfect. He didn't like anyone who was ugly, deformed or crippled, and she always had the horrible feeling that if she had been like that, he would have totally ignored her. Amy didn't understand much about politics, so had never had conversations with him about them.

Once Thomas had gone to university she only ever saw him during the holidays, but by that time she was wrapped up in her own circle of friends, and never mixed with him socially. Amy tried hard not to criticise her brother. She told Andrew Shaw that she was only concerned with Thomas deceiving the public and making a big show of helping people she knew he hated.

Andrew Shaw nodded again, and spoke to her.

"Thank you, Amy, you have been very helpful." He then fished in his pocket and brought out the coin they had given to David Clayton.

"This coin," he began, "is one of a few that Hitler had made, when he expected to win the war. There are none on the market, so they must be all in private hands. We will never know whether Hitler gave them to your grandmother as a gift, but as she was given the name of an antique dealer as a contact, I can only assume that he did give them to her with a view to her selling them if she fell on hard times. We feel, at this stage, that the coins belong to you, Amy. I don't know how much they are worth, but I should imagine it would be a very large sum." He smiled at Amy, and returned the coin to her.

Amy smiled back and looked at it carefully.

"Thank you Mr Shaw. I'm still not sure what to do with them," she replied.

Well," replied Andrew Shaw, "you could sell them and make yourself very rich, but then people would start asking you where you found them, or you could leave them locked in the bank for the time being, whilst you make up your mind."

I think I shall do that," she replied with a smile.

Andrew Shaw went on to speak about the researcher who was killed. "The hit and run appears to be genuine. I understand that no-one in Germany knows of your involvement, Amy, but it would not be difficult for some determined person to track down Joel."

"Mr, Shaw," asked Amy puzzled," are you going to investigate the hit and run in case it was murder?"

Andrew Shaw looked thoughtful for a moment, and smoothed his short red hair. "No, Amy, we are not." he replied.

"But why?" she exclaimed. Andrew Shaw looked at her.

"For your safety," he said quietly. Amy frowned, and Andrew Shaw continued.

"Amy, if this man was killed because he was tracing your ancestors, the last thing we want is for that person to know about you. If the killer has got away with murder (if it was murder) he may leave well alone, but if we start poking our noses in and muddying the waters, he may start looking for you and Joel." Amy nodded.

"You mean let sleeping dogs lie?" she asked thinking of David Clayton's remark

"Exactly," he replied.

Andrew Shaw wanted a few minutes alone with Joel. He looked at Amy and said, "Amy, would you kind enough to make us some coffee, before we leave?"

"Of course," she replied, and escaped to the kitchen.

Andrew Shaw spoke to Joel. "Mr Brent, I think you and Amy will be quite safe, but you do realise that we cannot give you both 24 hours a day protection?"

"Of course," replied Joel. Andrew Shaw passed Joel a piece of paper.

"If you or Amy ever feel in the slightest danger, or ever need any help, you can call me on any of these numbers and ask for me or my assistant, Peter Malcolm. In the meantime I want you to contact Charles in any emergency and take Amy to his home, his address is on this piece of paper. You can use Charles's home as a 'safe house' until we can get to you."

"Thank you very much," replied Joel, gratefully, putting the paper in his wallet.

Whilst he was taking some papers out of his briefcase, Andrew Shaw spoke to Joel.

"Can I ask you a personal question, Mr Brent?"

"Yes," replied Joel cautiously.

"Are you and Amy likely to marry?" Joel smiled.

"I'd love to marry Amy, but I couldn't ask her at the moment, it just isn't the right time. Why do you ask?"

"Because," replied Andrew Shaw slowly, "We feel that it may be rather unwise for Amy to have children." Joel interrupted.

"It's OK Mr Shaw, Amy has already decided that she will never risk having children. She is so afraid of getting pregnant, I'm living like a monk!" he grinned at the two men.

Andrew Shaw winked at Joel.

"I've been married many years, laddie, and I almost live like a monk!"

Charles Brown pulled a sad face and remarked.

"I'm a widower now, and I live like a monk all the time!" The three were laughing as Amy returned with a tray of coffee and biscuits.

"What are you lot laughing about?" she asked, pretending to be cross.

"Just men's talk, Amy," smiled Andrew Shaw, helping himself to coffee and biscuits. They all drank their coffee, and sat chatting. Before he left Andrew Shaw gave Amy and Joel the papers he had taken out of his briefcase.

"I shall have to ask you both to sign the Official Secrets Act," he said handing them both an official looking document. "Please read carefully before signing," he added.

Joel and Amy read through the forms.

"Goodness," cried Amy, "we could go to prison!"

"I'm sure it won't come to that Amy," said Andrew Shaw. "I don't suspect for one minute that you are going to tell anyone."

"Of course not," she replied, but it made her feel scared at the enormity of what they knew.

Joel and Amy signed the forms and gave them back to Andrew Shaw.

"Thank you, both," he smiled. "Charles has already signed one of these - in case you were worried."

As he and Charles Brown left, Andrew said to Amy.

"Now don't you worry about your brother, Amy, we'll keep a friendly eye on him. If what you say about him is true, we'll just make sure he doesn't get to Number 10."

When they had gone Amy and Joel sighed with relief.

"I can hardly believe what's happened," said Amy still amazed. "Just to think that I was so scared of Mr Brown, and he turns out to be such a nice man, who I can go to for help. And just to think that he knew my gran and her sister when they were young. He must have known all the places they went and what they did. He probably met their husbands, too. I wonder if he met Fransiska?"

Amy babbled on excitedly and Joel sat patiently and listened. He was more concerned about Thomas Kendal. What steps would they take to stop him ever becoming Prime Minister, one day? He tried to dismiss some of his thoughts from his mind.

Joel never told Amy of his fears.

CHAPTER FIFTEEN
THE DEATH OF THOMAS KENDAL – MARCH 1991

Andrew Shaw and Peter Malcolm had organised their surveillance team well. Their men had been told that Thomas Kendal may be in danger, and they suspected someone close to him. The men were told not to approach him, but were to watch him discreetly and photograph every person he came into contact with, and every person who went to his house. The front and the back of the house were to be watched. Thomas's telephone was tapped and only Andrew Shaw and Peter Malcolm were to listen to the tapes.

By the end of January nothing had been discovered. Thomas had not met anyone suspicious or made or received any phone calls that could give them a clue.

The Prime Minister was not sure whether to be angry or pleased. He had a high regard for Thomas, but at the same time was appalled that he was the grandson of Adolf Hitler.

At the beginning of February Thomas and Joanna went on holiday for three weeks to the Bahamas. Andrew Shaw laid off his team of men until their return. In the meantime he and Peter Malcolm went over the tapes again and again.

Andrew Shaw sighed, and rubbed a hand over the gingery beard that was forming on his chin. "There must be someone he has contacted within the last few weeks. We've had another child killer found dead – a faulty gas fire again and three gay bars burnt down – one in York and two in Brighton - all looking like 'accidents'." Peter Malcolm lit a cigarette and inhaled deeply – he was also at a loss.

"Look at these," he sighed pointing to the photos. "Not one likely person. They are all colleagues and friends. The same goes for visitors to the house. The only people are friends of Thomas and his wife and tradesmen who go round the back door. We've got food deliveries from Harrods, a couple of visits from the plumber, the dustbin men and Joanna's dressmaker. They have all been checked out, and not one of them has a criminal record or come to our notice for the slightest misdemeanour."

"I know," replied Andrew Shaw tapping the list in front of him. "It's the same with the phone calls – friends, family, colleagues, two calls to the plumber and Joanna's dressmaker and hairdresser." Peter Malcolm frowned again.

"Do you think he could have a contact in the Houses of Parliament? He could see someone there daily."

Andrew Shaw rubbed his chin again. "Well, we can't do much about that. We just couldn't keep every MP and member of staff under surveillance or tap hundreds of phones. I think we will have to fix a bug to the house. Thomas might just get careless if he is in his own house. We'll fix it to the living room wall."

"Good idea," replied Peter Malcolm. "We can get it done whilst he's away. I'll get our best man on it – it shouldn't be too difficult at the moment, as the gardener hasn't appeared yet, after the winter."

The 'bug' was planted before Thomas and Joanna returned from their holiday. Once they were home their men would watch the house and when, preferably in the evening when it was dark, Thomas was in the living room at the front of the house, Andrew Shaw would be contacted and he and Peter Malcolm would arrive in the 'van' and listen. They could not risk anyone else listening to the tapes.

Whilst Thomas and Joanna were still away Andrew Shaw and Peter Malcolm got to work on the "list" of Caroline Kendals contacts. Andrew Shaw had written out the names and addresses from the list and had given them to two members of his staff to try and trace. The first report was now ready.

Andrew Shaw and Peter Malcolm sat in the privacy of Andrew's office and Andrew began to read out the results. "First of all, Peter, we've got some information on the doctor, Peter Michaels. It appears that his family came over from Germany at the turn of the century. His father was a doctor at the German Hospital in Hackney and Peter Michaels also worked there after his training. It seems that in 1939 he suddenly came into money and moved to Harley Street. Now Peter Michaels was also a

ialified dentist and specialised in repairing people's faces after
ir crashes and accidents.

"Well, well, how convenient!" sneered Peter Malcolm.

"Quite," replied Andrew Shaw. "It seems that he retired in
)65 – no trace. We'll get our people to check further afield on
is one. The next one is Theodore Schen. He also came over from
:rmany. He arrived about 1910 and worked as a barman in
fferent East End pubs. In 1938 he suddenly gets 'promoted'
id becomes the Landlord of the Golden Lion, a haunt for many
:rman immigrants. On 1st November 1944 he was killed when
e pub was bombed, and here is a copy of his death certificate
im the General Register Office."

"So," replied Peter Malcolm the two of them came over from
:rmany before the First World War. They could have been
ying and helping Germany through two world wars. God, how
uld they have been missed!"

Andrew Shaw continued. "We now come to the Cropwell lot!
e first one, Harold Steel, the antique dealer, lived at Cropwell
inor, the local VIP. His family has lived there for years and
rold was Master of the local hunt. He had two children, who
d their own private tuition, and guess who their teacher was?"

"Let, me guess," grinned Peter Malcolm, "how about Gerald
iith?"

"Exactly!" exclaimed Andrew Shaw. Anyway, Harold Steel
d in 1980, copy of death certificate enclosed. His eldest son
v owns and lives in the Manor.

"What about the school teacher?" urged Peter Malcolm.

"Gerald Smith was born in 1912 in Leicester. He went to
idon University between 1930 and 1932. He taught Harold
el's children until they went to a boarding school, then he
ved to Bishops Fell school to await the beautiful Caroline!"

"What happened to him, Andrew?" queried Peter Malcolm.

"He retired in 1977 – no trace.

"What have we got on the solicitor?" urged Peter Malcolm
ting another cigarette.

"James Harrison was born in 1910 in Warwick. He went to
don University between 1928 and 1932. He moved to
pwell to begin a partnership with Collins and Hammond. They

131

are all dead now, and the solicitors are now Collins and Hodgekiss. James Harrison died in 1986, death certificate enclosed."

Peter Malcolm looked at Andrew Shaw. "Quite a little bunch of traitors in Cropwell we've got here, and they are all connected, one way or another." He stroked his hand across his neat crinkly hair, and looked thoughtful. "Do you think this Caroline was a spy?"

Andrew Shaw nodded his head slowly. "Aye, I wondered myself about that. The four of them could have quite something going in a little place like Bishops Fell. They could have had a radio hidden in that school, and people. They could have had meetings there. Caroline Kendal's letters were delivered by hand, the school could have been used as an information exchange and for deliveries. I would have thought though, that if she had been a spy she would have returned to Germany after the war."

"I don't suppose we will ever know," said Peter Malcolm sadly.

"True," replied Andrew Shaw. Well, I'll get our team to trace these last two, that's Peter Michaels and Gerald Smith. If they are both dead we'll send their names to the War Crimes Bureau, and they can put them on their file. If they are both still alive we'll get them watched and take it from there."

"Are you going to tell Amy Kendal?" asked Peter Malcolm.

"No, replied," Andrew Shaw, "and if she asks we'll tell her they are all dead."

It was 3rd March before Andrew Shaw got the first call from one of his watchers, to say that Thomas and Joanna were both at home, and in the living room. With a rush of excitement Andrew Shaw and Peter Malcolm got into the 'van' and drove off to Knightsbridge, and parked a few yards down the street. They settled down, put on their headphones, and waited, fingers hovering over the record button.

Thomas and his wife were sitting in their living room watching the news on TV. The living room, like the rest of the house was beautifully decorated in tasteful colours with the most expensive of furnishings. The velvet curtains were drawn across the windows, a fire glowed, and the chandeliers sparkled in the soft lights.

Thomas was lounging on the settee with his arm across anna's shoulders, stroking her neck. As they watched the news omas's face appeared on the screen. He had been televised rlier in the day visiting an old lady in hospital, who had been dly beaten up by her grandson, who had robbed her of her nsion, as he needed money for drugs. Thomas hated drug dicts and was genuinely sorry for the old lady. Thomas had ered to pay for the old lady to have a nice holiday when she ne out of hospital and to have her home redecorated. The nouncer was now saying that Thomas Kendal was now being led 'Saint Thomas' for all his good works.

"Darling," cried Joanna, stroking Thomas's leg, "You really marvellous!"

"Thank you, my sweet," replied Thomas smugly.

"Don't you think the old lady should go into a home?" asked nna.

"Oh, no," replied Thomas. "She's normally quite fit for her , and she is an intelligent woman. She will be alright to go k home."

"Have they caught the grandson yet?" his wife asked.

"Yes, "replied Thomas getting angry. "The little swine's in tody.

"Are you going to do anything about him?" she asked etly.

"I certainly am," growled Thomas, "His days are numbered."

"What have you got planned?" she queried, stroking back nds of golden hair from her eyes.

Thomas patted her hand. "You know that beautiful old nsion in Walthamstow that's opening up as a treatment centre drug addicts?" he asked.

"Yes," she replied, "the one you are angry about?"

"That's the one," he replied. Thomas started to raise his e. "Angry! I'm furious!" he exploded, shaking a fist in the air. e government have spent millions refurbishing a beautiful estral home for a bunch of bloody drug addicts. It's a race! The money should have been spent on it for decent ple who need help. And what to they do? They spend it on the m of the earth, and when they send that old lady's grandson there, his next 'fix' will be his last!" Thomas was shaking with rage.

"Good for you darling," replied Joanna, her blue eyes shining at Thomas, as he got up and started to pace the floor.

"That's not all," stormed Thomas. I've been asked to go to the opening with that disgusting pop singer Nico Tolly – God he's revolting! With his long greasy hair, earrings in every orifice he can find, and his dirty scruffy clothes. He's been bragging to the newspapers that he has been cured of the filthy habit of taking drugs, which is why he has been asked to attend the opening. They even expect me to shake his hand – I hope to God he hasn't got AIDS!"

Joanna took hold of his arm to calm him down. "Never mind, Thomas, you can always wash your hands afterwards," she teased.

"What I'd like to do, sneered Thomas, "Is to get a gun and shoot that piece of shit straight between the eyes!"

"Why don't you?" murmured Joanna.

"No, no, it would be too obvious. Don't worry I've got something good in store for that bunch of junkies".

Joanna eased Thomas back onto the settee and got them both a drink. The men in the van heard the chink of glasses. They looked at each wordlessly, the hairs on the backs of their necks standing on end.

"What are you going to do to them all?" asked Joanna not wanting to let the matter drop.

"It's best you don't know, Darling, the less you know the better. There was silence for a while until Joanna spoke again.

"What else have you got on the agenda, Thomas?" Thomas smiled.

"I've got a good one lined up for June."

"What is it?" she asked eagerly."

"Well," he replied," you know Edward and Poppy who have got all that land up in Yorkshire?"

"Of course," she replied.

"Well," he continued, "on 21st June, midsummer day, there
e thousands of gypsies going up there for one of their 'get
gethers', and Edward is renting out a couple of his fields. I told
m he must be mad, but he said they were paying him a lot of
oney."

"Stolen money, I expect," retorted Joanna.

"Quite," replied Thomas. "Now I understand that
derneath those fields are some old mine workings, so on that
ght there is going to be a nice little 'bang' and those fields are
ing to collapse, taking all those horrible gypsies with them"

"Thomas that's marvellous!" beamed Joanna, but what
out Edward and Poppy, we don't want them involved or
rmed.

"Don't worry about them, Darling, it so happens that it is
ppy's birthday on 21st June, and as she loves the theatre I have
oked seats for us all at the theatre to see Miss Saigon. They
l stay the night with us after the show. Edward knows, but I
s leaving it as a surprise for you and Poppy."

"Oh, Thomas, that's a wonderful idea," smiled Joanna
ppily, "you think of everything."

"Gotcha" whispered Andrew Shaw in the darkness of the
n'

"The murdering bastard," muttered Peter Malcolm, his heart
nding with the shock. His raised his eyebrows at Andrew
w.

"That bitch is just as bad. Would you believe it, and you
uldn't think that butter would melt in her mouth."

"He's got to be stopped," whispered Andrew Shaw, "and the
ner the better. Christ, what a nightmare!" He ran his fingers
ough his short red hair, still hardly able to believe what he
just been hearing. The atmosphere in the 'van' was tense.

All went quiet. Joanna went across to the drinks cabinet to
them both another drink. Thomas sat relaxed and began to
k about the first of his devoted 'disciples'.

Ever since the Kendals had lived in their Knightsbridge
se they had had their own maintenance man, Jack Oliver. He
been recommended by their neighbours who all used his
ices. Jack was a 'treasure'. He could turn his hand to

anything: plumbing, electrics and gas. Jack Oliver was a happy-go-lucky little Cockney, who lived in a little terraced house in Stepney, near the docks. He was in his 40's, small, wiry, and fit with light brown hair and grey eyes, a non-descript little man, who always wore blue denim overalls and an old cap. Jack was an honest hard-working man. He worked for himself – never got into trouble and always paid his VAT for being self-employed. Jack's greatest loves in his life were his sweet, plump little wife, Sally and his beautiful little daughter, Jackie. Jackie was an adorable child with big brown eyes like her mother and long shining brown hair, which she wore tied up in a pony tail. Jack always carried a photo of his 'Little Angel' in his pocket, and showed it to everyone.

One day Jack's little girl was abducted, raped and strangled. Jack and his wife, Sally were utterly heartbroken. The killer was a local man, Eric Bates, who was a tall thin, seedy looking man with thin features and long greasy hair. He had a record of molesting children and had been seen talking to the child, by a neighbour. Eric Bates was soon arrested and charged. Jack's wife became so distressed at the death of her precious child, that she committed suicide by taking an overdose of sleeping tablets. Now Jack had lost the two people he had loved most in the world.

All he had to live for was to see Eric Bates go to Prison for life. But that was not to be – for half way through the trial Eric Bates was released on a technicality – Jack was devastated.

Jack was so upset, he didn't know where to turn. In desperation he went to see Thomas Kendal, who he affectionately called Mr K. When Thomas saw the state that Jack was in, he ushered him into his study and gave him a stiff drink. Thomas was deeply sorry for Jack, a decent, ordinary, little man who always looked so at home in his cap and overalls. Jack was crying into his whisky.

"Oh, Mr K. I just want to kill that bastard with me own 'ands."

"Well," said Thomas softly, "why don't you?"

Jack looked up at Thomas in amazement, his red swollen eyes shining with hope.

"Do you think I could?" he asked huskily, looking intensely at Thomas.

"The man's a pervert and a drunk. It wouldn't be difficult to give him a little push as he is staggering past the Thames," Thomas murmured seductively.

Jack sat still for a moment, then looked up at Thomas. "Mr K. I'll bleedin' well do it!"

Before Jack left Thomas offered to give him an alibi if he was suspected.

"Mr K. You're a gent, a bleedin' gent, an' you just save me life."

Now that Jack was living alone he would go down to his local pub in the evening for a couple of pints. Sometimes he would have a hot meat pie there, for his supper and sometimes he would go to the chip shop and buy fish and chips, on his way home.

Jack knew where Eric Bates hung out. There had been a public outcry when he had been released. No one would speak to him or go near him. Most nights he sat alone in a pub and got drunk. One cold misty night Jack slipped out, unnoticed, from his local and made his way to the 'Anchor', where Eric would normally be found. Jack waited outside in the shadows until he saw Eric tottering out. Jack followed him slowly and quietly, hidden by the mist. They got to a low bridge over the river Thames. There was no-one about. Jack went up behind him and swiftly hoisted him up on to the low wall and gently pushed him over into the dark water. He landed with a gentle splash and the river swept him away.

Jack calmly walked away, and went back to his local. Nobody had even noticed that he had been out.

Eric's body was found the next day. The result at the inquest was 'accidental death' as it was believed that he fallen into the river whilst drunk. Nobody cared and nobody asked any questions.

Jack went to see Thomas. "It was easy Mr K." Thomas patted him on the back.

"Feeling better now, Jack?" he asked.

"I feel great, Mr K." he looked up at Thomas. "You got any more perverts I can bump off?" Thomas looked at Jack and frowned.

"Are you quite serious, Jack?" he asked.

"Course I am, Mr K. I just want to get revenge for me missus and Jackie."

"Right," said Thomas firmly, "There is a child molester being released in a couple of weeks from the Isle of Wight."

Jack grinned. "I just fancy a nice weekend by the sea."

"Come back in a week, Jack, and I'll give you the details – and, Jack, I'll pay you for this one."

A month later Jack went down to the Isle of Wight, and spotted his quarry. He followed him, unnoticed, in his little van. It took Jack a second to push the man off Beachy Head. By the time his body was found Jack was back in London.

Thomas and Jack formed a good partnership. When Thomas had a 'job' he would ring Jack to say that he had a problem with the plumbing or the electrics and Jack would go round to Thomas's.

They would go down to the cellar, where the fuses were, and would discuss the 'jobs' Thomas paid Jack well and Jack put the money away, never spending any of it. He saved it for his retirement. He wanted to buy a cottage by the sea to be near his sister.

After a while Jack would do other Jobs for Thomas. He could walk unnoticed into any building in his overalls and carrying his tool bag, without being questioned. Jack could 'fix' anything.

"Thomas," cooed Joanna, "You're daydreaming again – come along lets go to bed."

"But its only 10 o'clock," he replied, surprised.

"I said, bed, not sleep," she smiled at him seductively.

Thomas grinned, "How could a man turn down an offer like that" They both laughed.

Andrew Shaw and Peter Malcolm heard the door close. "Well, he's gone to get his leg over, we might as well pack up."

Peter Malcolm grinned. The two men stretched and yawned, then drove the 'van' back to the Special Branch Dept.

"This tape is dynamite," said Peter Malcolm awe-struck. I'll contact the P.M. in the morning – he'll have a fit when he hears it."

"Right, and I'll contact David Clayton."

The two men went into the office and locked the tape in Andrew Shaw's safe. "I need a drink," gasped Andrew Shaw, how about you, Peter?"

"Never felt the need more!" replied Peter Malcolm.

"We'll go to 'Victory' and I'll get our driver to pick us up from here and take us home!" replied Andrew Shaw.

The two men enjoyed a couple of stiff drinks and talked quietly about their 'problem'. Their driver eventually picked them up and took them home. Both men were deep in thought. The next morning Andrew Shaw contacted the Prime Minister, who agreed to see him and Peter Malcolm at 7p.m. that evening. They had an urgent meeting with David Clayton, and the three of them discussed the best way of getting rid of their 'problem', as the P.M. would want a quick decision, and they needed answers to all his possible questions.

At 7p.m. that evening Andrew Shaw and Peter Malcolm were once again in Howard Markham's office. The Prime Minister looked very worried as he asked, "What have you got for me Andrew?"

Andrew Shaw looked at the Prime Minister, his green eyes serious. "Evidence, Sir," and handed him the tape.

The Prime Minister took a deep breath, stroked his tie, and whispered, "Oh, God." He took the tape and put it in his machine. All three men sat in silence whilst the tape played. Howard Markham's face turned grey, and he looked sick. "This is monstrous," he whispered, his voice shaking. "It's unbelievable, and Joanna! My God, she's the daughter of Lord and Lady Westlake, and they are friends of the Royal Family!"

"What do you want us to do, Sir?" asked Andrew Shaw quietly.

Howard Markham looked at Andrew, "We still don't know who is working for him, but there is no time to waste. Do what is necessary, but don't touch his wife – it's too risky. Although she agrees with what he is doing, she doesn't take an active part, and she does not seem to know who Thomas employs, or anything else. Do you have a plan?"

Andrew Shaw and Peter Malcolm outlined their plan. The Prime Minister nodded. "Yes, I think it will work, and there will be no scandal, well done."

Howard Markham pulled himself together. He sat at his desk, hands clasped. He looked the two men straight in the eye. "Well, Gentlemen, we have one week before the opening of the home in Walthamstow, Kendrick House. What arrangements have you made?"

Andrew Shaw leaned forward. "We have got our team searching the house from top to bottom. They will take extra care in checking the heating systems and the electrics. When they have finished we shall keep the house under surveillance until the opening.

"Good," replied the Prime Minister. Now, do we know who Edward and Poppy are?"

Peter Malcolm spoke next. "Yes, sir, they are good friends of Thomas Kendal. Edward Lansdowne owns a mill up in West Yorkshire, it is a clothing mill. He also owns quite a lot of the surrounding land. We are having it checked out to see where the old mines are situated. When we have the plans we shall check all the mine entrances to see if any of them have been entered. If not we shall keep them watched right up until the 21st June."

"Excellent," replied Howard Markham. "I will leave this in your hands, Andrew, and keep me informed."

"Naturally, Sir," answered Andrew Shaw.

The two men left Downing Street, taking the tape with them.

The Prime Minister sat at his desk. He buried his head in his hands.

The opening of Kendrick House was in the newspapers the following week. It showed pictures of the pop singer, Nico Tolly, looking thin and lined with his unshaven face, greasy hair and scruffy clothes. There had been a protest in the papers about him being at the opening, but the 'do gooders' had insisted that as he had overcome the 'habit' he would be a good example to others.

The 13th March was cold and frosty. Thomas was taken to the ɔpening of Kendrick House by his faithful chauffeur, Albert and ʽNico Tolly was taken in a Rolls Royce by his chauffeur. When hey arrived they were surrounded by TV cameras and crowds of ɔeople, who were more interested in the notorious Nico Tolly, han the opening of Kendrick House. Thomas and Nico were ɡreeted by a council official along with the Head of the new drugs ɛentre, Dr Challis and some of his staff. Introductions were made. Thomas looked smart in a dark, expensive overcoat, his ʄair hair shining and his blue eyes watching the crowd, trying to ʄide the distaste of meeting Nico Tolly, who disgusted him so much. Nico Tolly was grinning and waving at the crowd. His hair ʄad been washed and was tied back in a ponytail. He had ʃhaved. Earrings glinted in his eyebrows, nose, ears, and tongue. ʃe was dressed in black leather covered in silver studs, and long ʄlack high-heeled boots.

Before going into the home everyone was standing at the top f the flight of steps outside the main door. As requested Thomas ɳd Nico Tolly shook hands and turned to face the TV cameras ʄefore going inside. At that moment there was a slight hiss, and ʄhomas Kendal sank to the floor. He had been shot between the yes!

Blood seeped from Thomas's head and ran down his ʄandsome face. Someone screamed, and suddenly all hell was let ʄose. Someone shouted, "Call the police – get an ambulance!" Dr. ʄhallis, the Head of the new centre, bent down beside Thomas, ʄlthough he knew there was nothing he could do. The office staff ʄragged the trembling Nico Tolly into the building. He was white ʄith shock. Officials and two on duty uniform policemen kept the ʄowd at bay. Some of them screaming, some of them in a silent ʄate of shock.

Within minutes sirens were heard and three police cars and ʄ ambulance arrived. The area was cordoned off and the police ʄok over. The cameras were filming everything. Albert, got out of ʄhomas's car, threw a half-smoked cigarette to the floor, and ran ʄ the scene horrified, unable to believe what had happened to ʄs beloved master.

Thomas's body was eventually taken away by the ʄnbulance. The area was searched for the gunman – he was ever ʄund.

141

A policeman and a policewoman were sent to Thomas's home to tell Joanna before the news reached the television. The filming of the opening of Kendrick House was not live, but was being filmed for the evening news.

When the police arrived at Thomas's house, the door was opened by the housekeeper, Hannah, as Albert had not yet returned home. He had, in fact, followed the ambulance to the morgue. Hannah showed the police into the living room where Joanna was sitting. She stood up at the sight of them, pushing strands of golden hair behind her ears. "Is there something wrong?" she asked haughtily.

The policeman told her gently what had happened. Joanna turned as white as sheet and then became hysterical. She screamed and screamed. "No!No! No!" The policewoman asked the shocked Hannah to send for the doctor and Thomas's private secretary Giles Harper. Hannah went off to the telephone in tears, whilst the policewoman, went over to Joanna to try and comfort her.

Tears poured down Joannna's white face, and she was trembling from head to foot. She shook her head in disbelief and horror. Had Thomas changed his mind about shooting Nico Colly? Had the gunman missed and hit Thomas by mistake? Joanna was too terrified to think straight!

The doctor soon arrived after hearing the dreadful news from Hannah. He and the policewoman took Joanna up to her bedroom, where she was sedated. Giles Harper arrived soon afterwards. He was a tall slim young man with neat brown hair and wearing horn-rimmed glasses. Giles was deeply shocked, but being efficient and sensible he took soon charge of the bewildered household. He sent for Joanna's best friend, Lady Sarah Armstrong, to come and stay with her. He then had to ring Henry and Penny and Joanna's parents. The two police officers stayed at the house to keep the awaited press from the door.

Joanna's parents, on being told the news agreed to come down to London to be with their daughter. They would be arriving during the evening.

When Giles finally got hold of Henry, he was still at school. The Headmaster was deeply distressed at the terrible news and told Henry to go home. Henry, got in his car, and in a daze, drove to the department store to tell Penny and take her home. When

Henry told Penny that Thomas had been killed, she fainted with shock, and was taken to the staff sickroom. Penny was white, as she came round she looked at Henry, he hazel eyes filled with pain. "Tell me it's not true," she whispered, Henry's eyes were full of tears.

"I'm sorry, Pen." His voice was husky with emotion.

The manageress was marvellous. She sent out for hot sweet tea, put her arms round Penny and tried to comfort her. She sat with them both until Henry felt able to take Penny home. When they got home, Henry rang for their doctor. Penny seemed to have gone into a trance, and he didn't know what to do. He suddenly remembered Amy – he dreaded having to tell her. He rang the bank and spoke to Joel, who agreed to tell Amy, and bring her to the house.

Joel went to find Amy and took her to his office. "What's wrong, Joel," she asked puzzled, seeing the worry in his eyes. Joel put his hands on her shoulders, and said, quietly,

"Amy, your father rang. I'm afraid it's Thomas, he's been killed." Amy looked at him in astonishment. "Killed! What on earth has happened?"

"I don't know exactly, but your father needs you. Your mother has taken it very badly." The colour had drained from Amy's face. With trembling legs she fetched her bag and coat and followed Joel to his car. Amy was numb with shock, and sat silent all the way to her parent's home. When they arrived they got out of the car, and Joel put his arm round her and they walked to the front door. Henry opened it as they arrived.

"Thank God you're here!" croaked Henry.

"Dad, what's happened?" cried Amy, as she rushed into his arms.

"There's just been a newsflash on the TV," said Henry "Thomas was at the opening of a new drugs centre in Walthamstow, when he was shot. They think the shot was meant for some pop singer called Nico Tolly, who was with him, and Thomas got shot by mistake."

"Where's mum?" she asked urgently.

143

"She's upstairs. Waiting for the doctor," replied Henry, still in a daze. Amy raced up the stairs to be with her mother, who, she knew, would be devastated at the death of Thomas.

Joel stood with Henry watching the TV news, which was now full of the death of Thomas. "I'm truly sorry, Henry," said Joel kindly.

"I just can't believe it," replied Henry looking bewildered at Joel. They both turned back towards the television as a further news flash came on. It appeared that Nico Tolly had had some death threats during the previous week, and the police were certain that he was the real target, and the death of Thomas Kendal had been a terrible tragedy.

The doorbell suddenly rang. Henry went to the door to find their doctor, Bill Thomas standing on the doorstep. Bill Thomas, a small, dark-haired little Welshman, like many people in Cropwell, knew Henry and his family well. He had known Thomas and Amy since they were young children, and was very proud of Thomas's achievements. "Bill, thank God you are here!" cried Henry relieved.

"Henry, I am so sorry to hear about Thomas!" replied Bill, in his rich singsong voice.

"Bill, please come up and see Penny, I'm so worried about her" Henry took Bill Thomas up to see Penny who was lying on their bed in a daze, Amy holding her hand and crying. Bill went up to her and checked her pulse.

"She's in shock, Henry. I'll give her a sedative for now, and I'll come back in the morning." Bill filled a syringe from his bag, wiped her arm and gently pushed a syringe into it. Penny's eyes closed and she lay still.

Whilst Penny lay in a dreamless sleep, Henry, Amy and Bill Thomas made their way downstairs. Bill and Henry went into the living room to speak quietly to each other, whilst Amy went to the front door with Joel. Amy felt cold and couldn't stop shivering. Joel rubbed her shoulders and arms. "Joel," she whispered, "do you really thinks it was an accident?"

"Of course," he replied, "don't go blaming yourself, for what has happened." He hugged her tightly. "Amy, I have to get back to the bank, but I'll come back later," he said softly.

"Thanks, Joel," she replied tremulously. "I will have to go to the cottage and get some clothes and things. I shall stay here with Mum and Dad for a while."

"Of course," he agreed, "You must." He hugged her again. "I'll see you later, Amy." Amy stood in the doorway, a sad little figure, until Joel had driven away.

Meanwhile in Knightsbridge Giles was kept busy. Lady Sarah arrived in a taxi. She was Joanna's best friend. She looked very much like Joanna with her long blonde hair and blue eyes, but their personalities were quite different. Sarah was carefree and wild. With her long shapely legs she strode rather than walked. She smoked and drank and loved parties and late nights. She sailed into the house like a breeze smelling of Chanel. "Giles, you angel, where is she for God's sake!" she shouted.

"Up in her room, Sarah," he replied. She bounded up the stairs like a greyhound and swept into Joanna's room.

After the waves of Sarah's arrival had ebbed, Giles told Hannah that the Westlakes and their chauffeur would be arriving during the evening, and asked her to prepare rooms and a meal. Hannah went off tearfully to the kitchen and made everyone a strong cup of tea, including herself. Whilst they were drinking it Albert finally came home after officially identifying the body of Thomas. He was also very upset. He eventually agreed, after taking off his glasses and wiping his eyes, with Giles to answer the door and telephone calls, and take messages.

Joanna remained asleep upstairs, and every now again Lady Sarah would pop down for a quick drink and a 'ciggie'. They were all awaiting the arrival of Lord and Lady Westlake – Marcus and Emma. Although this couple were wealthy and well-known, they were always charming and polite to everyone, and were just as courteous to staff as they were to their own kind.

The evening was hectic with visitors and phone calls. Reporters were hanging about outside, and the television news was full of the tragic death of Thomas Kendal.

The Westlakes arrived at 9p.m. – a handsome couple. They were both in their 50's, tall and elegant. Marcus was a 'gentleman', who could only been described as a 'grey' person. From the top of his silver hair, grey eyes and moustache to his immaculate grey suit and dark grey shoes. He was a beautifully spoken and well mannered man. Emma was truly attractive for her age, with her shoulder length blonde immaculately groomed hair, blue eyes just like her daughter and a small, perfect nose and mouth, even her teeth looked too good to be true! She was dressed in a long brown wool skirt with a cream cashmere sweater, and gold chains hung round her slender throat. Her Christian Dior perfume floated behind her as she moved.

Their chauffeur brought in their luggage and Albert took it up to their rooms. Emma Westlake went straight upstairs to see her daughter, whilst her husband went into the living room with Giles where he was given a glass of whisky and a cigar. The Westlakes were to stay until after the funeral. An inquest was held a few days later, the verdict was as expected, murder by person or persons unknown. Once the inquest was over Giles made the funeral arrangements on behalf of the Westlakes. He contacted Henry with all the details. Henry and his family were to drive to Thomas's home to meet up with the Westlakes and wait for the funeral cars to take them to the church. After the service they would be taken to a nearby hotel where family and close friends would be given drinks and a hot buffet. When they were ready to go they would be taken back to Knightsbridge to pick up their car. The funeral was to take place the following Thursday at 3 p.m.

The day of Thomas's funeral was bitterly cold. It had started to snow and small flakes were whirling and dancing in the strong March wind.

Joel had agreed to take the Kendal's to the funeral, much to everyone's relief. He picked them up at 11 am. They had all wrapped up warmly. Henry and Penny sat in the back of the car. Penny was still in a bad way and looked dreadful. Her hazel eyes were pools of misery in a face that looked grey and lined. She seemed to have aged ten years in the last few days. Her dull, lifeless hair was covered in a silky black woollen hat, and her black clothes seemed to hang on her body. She clung to Henry like a child, holding onto his arm and burying her normal pretty face against his shoulder. Henry looking tired and strained gently patted her arm and held her close.

Amy also looked pale and tired, although she did look elegant in a long black tailored coat with a fur lined hood, long black boots and a fluffy black scarf around her throat. Joel had put the heater on his car and it was warm and comfortable.

Amy was silent on the drive to London. She watched the snowflakes tap the windscreen like white petals turning into crystals, only to be swept away by the windscreen wipers. Amy felt like those snowflakes – her life was being swept away beneath her feet. Finding that deed box of her grandmother's had been like opening Pandora's box. She turned her head to look out of the side window, and thought of her poor father sitting in the back of the car with her shell of a mother. All this tragedy and they didn't know even half the truth. Amy had tried to find out some of the family life of Adolf Hitler, her true grandfather, but she had not found much. He had been born on 20th April, 1889 at Braunau in Upper Austria, the son of a lesser customs official, originally called Schicklgruber. His parents died when he was young and he had been left a lonely orphan. He had lived a life of hardship between 1904 to 1910 in Vienna. He had become a draughtsman and moved to Munich in 1912. Amy shuddered. Had Hitler's lonely sad young life made him what he was? Or would he have been just an evil anyway? No matter how she tried, she could not erase the terrible truth from her mind.

Joel drove carefully along the wet roads. He would like to have played some classical music, and was tempted to put a tape in the machine in the car, but looking at the sad faces in his car he decided that the emotion in the music would be too much to bear, and Amy and her parents would have all been in tears. He stole a look at Amy, who was gazing out of the window with so much hurt in her eyes, he wanted to hold her and take away the pain.

They arrived at Thomas's home just before 2 O'clock. a good hour before the funeral. They drew up outside the front of the house. As they got out they were besieged by reporters, one of them pushing a microphone in front of Henry's face, and started asking him questions. Henry frowned and put up a hand, "I'm sorry," he replied firmly, "but we are too upset to talk to anyone." A policeman moved the reporters away, and the Kendals walked up the steps to the front door, where they were shown in by a sombre Albert.

As they entered the house the Westlakes greeted them. Emma walked over to them in a haze of expensive perfume.

"Henry, Penny, do come in and warm yourselves," she cried, ushering them both into the living room.

"Thank you, Emma," replied Henry gratefully.

"Amy, how are you, my dear, and is this your young man?" greeted Marcus Westlake.

"I'm fine thank you, Marcus, and this is Joel," she introduced. The two men shook hands, and they followed Henry and Penny into the living room. Giles welcomed the family warmly, and handed them all a drink. Emma guided the forlorn Penny to the sofa and rubbed her cold trembling hands between her own warm, bejewelled ones. The two women talked quietly together, Emma trying her best to console Penny. Hannah came in with a tray of tea and coffee and some dainty sandwiches and handed them round.

The Kendals were made very welcome and were fussed over by everyone. As the family of Thomas Kendal everyone knew what a terrible day it was for them. Joanna was up in her room with her friend Lady Sarah. Joanna had been so ill she had stayed in her room since the death of her husband.

Just before three o'clock everyone began to move into the hall. They all looked up as Joanna came slowly down the stairs with Sarah. Amy was shocked at the sight of her – she looked dreadful. Her face was white, showing up the black rings which circled her clouded eyes. Her hair was scraped back under a fur hat that completely covered her head, and her body was trembling under her matching fur coat. Joanna felt even worse than she looked. Apart from the shock of losing her husband she was suffering from morning sickness, which had started plaguing her just days before his death.

As she got to the bottom of the stairs her father, Marcus, took her other arm and moved her towards the Kendals, where she weakly whispered, "Hello, Henry, Penny, Amy."

The cortege drew up outside the house and Giles led everyone to their respective cars. The sight of Thomas's flower topped coffin in the hearse was too much for Penny, and she burst into tears. Henry and Joel took her by the arms and led her to the waiting limousine. Henry sat beside her as she sobbed. She had not been allowed, by Henry, to visit the undertakers and see

Thomas's body. It would have been too much for her. Amy and Joel joined them.

Joanna, too, broke down at the sight of her husband's coffin, and started to faint. Marcus and Giles managed to get her into her limousine, where she was comforted by her parents. Giles and Lady Sarah made their way to the third car and Albert and Hannah followed in Thomas's Rolls Royce. The procession moved off slowly to the church under grey skies and falling snow.

They arrived at the church a few minutes later, where there were crowds of people standing outside along with TV cameras and newspaper reporters. The Kendals and the Westlakes made their way through the crowd and into the church. Music was playing softly as they walked to the front of the church, where the Kendals sat on one side and the Westlakes on the other. Amy wondered if David Clayton and the men from Special Branch were there, but the church was packed, and she was afraid to look round.

Eventually Thomas's coffin glided up the aisle on the shoulders of the pallbearers and was laid gently on to the bier. The flowers lying on top of the coffin were breathtaking, and the smell unforgettable. The service began.

Amy was conscious of her mother's weeping beside her, as she listened to the service. She felt dreadful about the death of her brother. She remembered how kind he had been to her when she was a little girl. She never dreamt that something as awful as this could happen to him. Amy never knew what her brother had really been up to during his life, her only concern had been him becoming the Prime Minister and the grandson of Adolf Hitler, and the insincerity of his beliefs. She clutched Joel's hand during the service, thanking God that she found such a wonderful friend.

Amongst the congregation was Jack Oliver, looking totally unrecognisable in his smart winter coat and shiny black shoes. He, too, had been devastated by the death of Thomas. He had just heard about the deaths at Kendrick House, where most of the drug addicts in the clinic had died through poisoned drugs. Jack had had nothing to do with that. He had only taken the message to the house of a young nurse whose husband had been killed by a drug addict who had been high on drugs, stolen a car and smashed into her poor husband and killed him and their

149

baby son. Jack was now unsure what to do next, without Thomas, he had no guide. The service was long with different people, including the Prime Minister, coming to the front of the church, and making their tributes to Thomas. The words remembered by everyone were, 'Thomas Kendal, a saint in life – a saint in death.' Amy and Joel looked at each other wordlessly – no-one else in the church knew the evil behind Thomas's charm.

Amy could hardly believe how many people there were at Thomas's funeral, it was unnerving.

After the service the coffin was taken to the graveyard at the back of the church. Only family and closest friends were at the graveside. The sky was still grey and heavy, and now large snowflakes were falling covering the mourners' clothes and turning the trees into sparkling white sculptures. Amy wrapped her scarf round her face to stop the snowflakes falling into her eyes and mouth. She held Joel's hand tightly as the coffin was lowered into the cold, dark ground. Penny was clinging to Henry, and Joanna was clinging to her father. It was a very sad and unforgettable day.

Everyone was frozen, and when the cars finally deposited family and friends at the nearby Hilton Hotel, they all hurried inside to get warm. Glasses of sherry were handed to everyone as they entered the sumptuous bar. People started mixing and talking to each other. Emma insisted that Penny and Henry be introduced to some of Thomas's friends and colleagues. Penny felt like an old frump amongst all these rich, clever people, she had been too upset to even get her done or put on her make-up, but everyone was very kind to her.

Joanna was sitting in a window seat, being cared for by friends including Edward and Poppy Lansdowne, who had come down from Yorkshire. The opportunity gave Lady Sarah a chance to waltz off and get herself another drink, and light up a cigarette, which she waved in the air as she spoke to people. Amy and Joel looked at each other as if to say, "Who is that crazy woman?"

Eventually the guests moved into another room where a hot buffet had been laid out. There was soup, warm rolls, turkey, beef and jacket potatoes, followed by cheese and biscuits and coffee. The service was excellent, and the atmosphere had become warm and friendly.

After the buffet people wandered back into the bar for more
drinks, but as the weather was getting worse the Kendals decided
to leave. They said their goodbyes to the Westlakes and Thomas's
friends, and Albert took them back to Knightsbridge to collect
Joel's car.

By the time they left London it was dark, and it was
snowing harder. The wipers were fighting a battle with the white
enemy. The heater was on full blast to keep them all warm. Joel
drove carefully, his powerful car sweeping along the wet roads.
Penny fell asleep in the back of the car, her head on Henry's
shoulder. Amy sat in the passenger seat, thoughtful. There was
so much she wanted to say to Joel, but not in front of her
distraught parents.

The Westlakes did not stay long after the Kendals had gone.
Joanna felt so unwell, her parents took her home and put her to
bed.

The funeral over, Joanna decided to return to the Lake
District with her parents. She was very frightened after the
murder of Thomas, and wanted to get away from London and
never come back. Her mother helped her to pack some clothes to
take with her, and Hannah agreed to pack the rest of her
belongings, and she and Albert would bring them up to Westlake
Manor. Giles would arrange for the sale of the house, and Albert
and Hannah would stay on as caretakers for the time being.

The fall of snow did not last, and in a couple of days it had
cleared enough for the Westlakes to make their journey home.

By the time Joanna had settled herself in her parents home,
she realised she was pregnant. She eventually told her parents,
who were delighted, but not so happy when Joanna insisted that
her in-laws were not to be told.

The Kendals never knew.

CHAPTER SIXTEEN
18 MONTHS LATER – SEPTEMBER 1992

It was a beautiful September. The mornings awakened to a soft mist shrouding the countryside, slowly rising to reveal a warm, sunny day, with a soft breeze blowing the falling leaves.

Up in the Lake District, Thomas Kendal junior was sitting in his nursery, playing with his toy bricks. He was watched over by his nanny and his adoring mother. Thomas was a beautiful child with his father's sapphire eyes and his mother's golden hair. He was adored by everyone. The only family he knew was his mother and his maternal grandparents.

The Westlakes were not happy about deceiving Henry and Penny, and denying the little boy his paternal grandparents and his Aunt Amy. "He'll find out one day, and may not forgive you," Emma had warned her daughter.

Down in Cropwell the weather was glorious. The Kendals had got over the shock of their son's death and were looking forward to the marriage of their only daughter, Amy to Joel.

It had taken Joel some time to persuade Amy to marry him, as she thought it unfair that he should marry her when she could not risk giving him any children. "Amy," Joel had insisted, "if you don't marry me, I won't marry anyone else, so I won't have any children anyway."

Amy loved Joel very much. He was her soul-mate, her rock. How she would ever had coped without him during the last couple of years she couldn't imagine. "What if I get pregnant?" she kept asking him.

"Amy, if we both take precautions, you won't, and if we did have an 'accident' you could have a termination. I know it wouldn't be nice, but I would agree."

Amy had finally given in and arrangements were made. As there was not enough room in the cottage for all Joel's belongings they finally agreed to live in Joel's flat during the week, as it was nearer the bank, and live in the cottage at weekends. Joel told

Amy that could she decorate and refurnish the flat however she wished, which she did with great enjoyment.

The wedding day had arrived. It was quite an event as there were not many weddings in Bishops Fell. Penny was happy and excited, and looked lovely in a blue suit that set of her new hair style, which was now cut in a shining bob, in a rich brown. Henry was a little nervous, but looked confident and handsome in his morning suit.

Joel's parents were thrilled about the wedding. He was the last of their children to marry. The men all looked handsome in their morning suits. Joel's mother, Maria, looked gorgeous in a yellow dress and jacket with a matching hat on her sleek black hair, Her brown eyes were shining as she looked at her handsome son, who, like her other children, had inherited her Italian looks.

Joel's brother, James was at the wedding with his wife, Helen, who was expecting their second child. Joel's sister Sofia was with her husband, Mark. Their two little girls were the bridesmaids, who were excited and happy in their long peach dresses and satin shoes. They arrived at the church holding small baskets of peach flowers, and kept jumping up down and tugging at Joel's hands.

Joel's uncle, James, was also at the wedding, another banker, with his wife Charlotte and their grown up children, James junior who was a student and their daughter, Rachel, who worked in a forensic laboratory near London. Rachel had always liked her cousin Joel, and liked his best man even more! Joel's best man was Neil Smart, a long-life friend of Joel's who was a petty officer in the Royal Navy. He would often visit Joel when he was on leave and had grown very fond of Amy. He winked at the blushing Rachel as they all moved into the church.

Amy looked as beautiful as any bride could be. She looked lovely in a dress of white lace and frills, with a head-dress of pearls on her shining hair. She drove the short journey with her father in a horse and carriage.

Everyone enjoyed the wedding of Amy and Joel. They were a handsome couple, and a very special couple. They had a special closeness with the sharing of Amy's terrible secret that no one would ever know.

After the service Amy and Joel posed for photographs, and
then, to everyone's delight, walked from the church to the Kings
Head for their reception, which was in an upstairs room. The
room was old with heavy oak beams, tiny mullioned windows and
an uneven floor. The room had been decorated with masses of
flowers, and a magnificent wedding cake stood on a small table in
the corner. The wedding tables were laid with flowers, sparkling
glasses, shining cutlery, and napkins in peach to match the
bridesmaids' dresses.

The wedding party was small, consisting of Henry and
Jenny, the Brents and a number of friends including Molly and
Richard, Henry's next-door neighbours. The meal was excellent
and the champagne flowed.

After the reception Joel and Amy went to the cottage to get
changed and Joel's brother James and his wife, drove them to the
airport to catch a flight to America where they were to join a ship
for a 3 week cruise.

Amy and Joel were excited and happy. Their fears and
troubles were over, and as long as they kept silent there should
be no more problems. They travelled first class on the plane, and
stayed in marvellous hotel for their first night.

The following day they joined their cruise ship the 'Orlando'.
Their luggage was taken from them on their arrival and they
waited in a departure lounge and were given boarding tickets.
They sat and waited for their turn to be called. Amy was as
excited as a child, waiting for her first Caribbean cruise. Their
numbers were called and they moved through the doorway where
their photograph was taken. They then walked up the gangplank
where they met by their cabin steward who took them to their
room, the honeymoon suite. It was beautiful with a king size
canopied bed and a suite of expensive furniture, and a huge
basket of flowers for Amy.

Amy and Joel enjoyed a wonderful honeymoon. They were
waited on hand and foot. They ate and drank and sunbathed on
deck. They visited wonderful places and bought gifts to take
home. They made many friends and laughed and joked. Amy had
never been so happy.

Her life felt perfect.

Back in Cropwell, everything was getting back to normal.

Henry and Penny were feeling happier than they had for some time, and Penny was looking forward to having grandchildren now that Amy was married.

One Sunday, whilst Amy was still on her honeymoon, Henry was in the back garden mowing the lawn. It was a lovely sunny autumn day, and he was feeling content and relaxed. He heard the phone ring in the house, but left Penny to answer it. A moment later she came to the back door. "Henry," she called, "there is an American lady on the phone for you."

"American?" asked Henry. "Who is she?"

"I've no idea, but she wants to talk to you," she replied.

Henry walked through the kitchen and into the hall, and picked up the phone. "Hello," he said, puzzled. An American voice spoke.

"Am I speaking to Henry Kendal?" she drawled.

"Yes," replied Henry, "how can I help you?"

"Henry, were you born on 1st March, 1942?"

"Yes, I was," replied Henry, more puzzled that ever.

"Well," she continued, "You don't know me, but my name is Fransiska Jeffries, and I am looking for my long lost little brother, and I think you may be able to help me . . .

If you have enjoyed this book, look out for the
sequel:

Sleeping Dogs II

Coming soon!